"Are you all right?" the man asked

She lifted her head, but before she could answer, her car door was wrenched open. "Why the hell didn't you— You!"

Maxine's eyes widened in shocked disbelief as she stared into the eyes of Kurt Raynor. What was he doing here, so near her home?

"Why didn't you answer me?" he demanded. "I thought you were injured."

Her eyes closed of their own accord. Her voice was very small as she spoke. "N-no, I'm—I'm okay."

"You're sure?"

She opened her eyes, looking up at his grim features with a shudder. It had been so close . . . that feeling of being out of control. "I'm sure." She waited then for an explosion of temper, for recriminations, accusations. None came.

"Get out, Miss Smith." It was a quiet command.

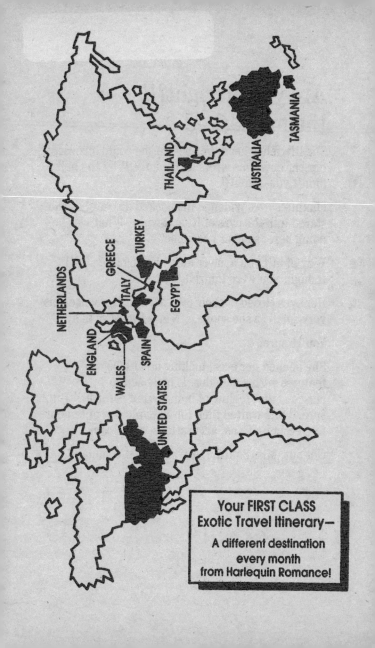

NETHERLANDS
ENGLAND
WALES
GREECE
ITALY
TURKEY
SPAIN
EGYPT
THAILAND
AUSTRALIA
TASMANIA
UNITED STATES

Your FIRST CLASS
Exotic Travel Itinerary—

A different destination
every month
from Harlequin Romance!

AN ANSWER FROM THE HEART

Claudia Jameson

Harlequin Books

TORONTO • NEW YORK • LONDON
AMSTERDAM • PARIS • SYDNEY • HAMBURG
STOCKHOLM • ATHENS • TOKYO • MILAN

Original hardcover edition published in 1990
by Mills & Boon Limited

ISBN 0-373-03159-9

Harlequin Romance first edition November 1991

For Marlene and Roger Michael, with love.
Love is all there is.

AN ANSWER FROM THE HEART

Printed in U.S.A.

CHAPTER ONE

'Is THAT you, Maxine? I'm in the dining-room.'

Maxine Smith let herself into the house with a sigh, glad to be home, grateful for the warmth of the central heating. It was freezing outside; the drive from work was so short that the heater in her car hadn't had time to warm up. It was Monday and it had been a bad day all around.

'I'm in here.'

'I heard you the first time, Polly. Be with you in a minute.' Maxine had not needed to be told where her sister was, she had seen her when she'd pulled on to the drive; the dining-room was at the front of the house, the living-room and the kitchen at the back. 'I'm just putting the kettle on.'

'I'm sure it'll suit you!'

That old joke. How many times had she and Polly said that to one another? Countless. She sighed again, picked up the kettle and put it down, changing her mind. Something stronger was in order right now, and she reached into a kitchen cupboard and took out a bottle of brandy and a glass.

'What's the matter? You look...have you been sacked or something?'

Maxine glanced at her sister and sank on to a chair. Sacked or something? Polly thought that was a joke; she was sitting at the dining table, checking the bank statement as she did every month. It was her task to pay all the bills, to keep their finances in order—not that Maxine was incapable, far from it. Hadn't her

boss told her often that she was the best secretary a
man could have? It had taken some time for her to
believe that, though; it had been very difficult to fill
Miss Ainsley's shoes. Maxine's predecessor had
worked for John Dunn for years and years, and
Maxine had been only nineteen when she had taken
over from her. Still, she was good; when it came to
secretarial work or anything to do with figures, she
was good.

'Not quite.' She put the glass and the bottle on the
table and poured herself a stiff drink, aware of her
sister's astonishment.

'What on earth—are you ill?'

'I'm not ill.'

'Then why the brandy? At this hour? It isn't like
you to——'

'I know. Look, I'm cold and tired and...' She might
just as well come right out with it, why beat about
the bush? It was depressing but it wasn't the end of
the world. 'And I haven't exactly been sacked but—
well, it might be as bad as that. Mr Dunn is selling
up.'

'*Selling up?* What—I mean how——?'

Maxine held up a hand. 'I know what you mean.
I was just as shocked, you can imagine. I *knew* something strange was going on! Didn't I say to you a week
ago that Mr Dunn had been acting oddly?' He had
been acting very oddly, in fact. There had been several
occasions when he had asked Maxine to leave his office
when he'd taken phone calls, which was something
he didn't normally ask of her, and there had been his
mysterious disappearances from the premises, when
he had never told her where he was going or how long
he would be.

'Yes, but you laughed about it, Max. You thought——'

'I thought he'd met someone.' There was a wry smile. That her boss had suddenly acquired a lady-friend had been her best guess. 'I thought he was being mysterious because he had a dark secret. Well, he had—but it had nothing to do with a woman. It had to do with a take-over. No sooner had I got in this morning than he called me into his office. I knew something was up. He looked grave, apologetic. At first I thought he was unwell but he was far from it. When he dropped his bombshell about the take-over he looked delighted. Oh, he apologised—he apologised profusely about being so secretive, even with me, or especially with me, as he put it. He said he hadn't dared to let anyone know anything until his negotiations with the new owner were complete. He said he was afraid it would all fall through if he told anyone, that he felt a sort of superstition he couldn't really make sense of.' She broke off, sighing again. 'I knew what he meant, I understood it, but it didn't lessen the shock. Anyhow, he went on to say that he wanted me to be the first to know, as if it were wonderful news.'

'I suppose it is, for him.' It was Polly's turn to sigh. 'That heart attack really frightened him, didn't it?'

The younger girl nodded slowly. That was what had brought this about; her boss had had a heart attack nine months earlier, had spent weeks off work recovering. Lately he had seemed well enough, if not exactly his old self—and that was another thing, he was sixty-two years old, as he had pointed out only this morning, several times, and getting out of the business was the only sensible thing for him to do. It was, too; it could kill him otherwise. It was just that

Dunn & Dunn Limited seemed to have been around forever. They were, or rather they had been, a family business, and John Dunn was all that was left of that family except for his only child, who had emigrated long since.

'Yes, it really frightened him.' Maxine hardly knew how to continue; she had told her sister the bad news but there was worse to come. 'I—what I don't understand is *how* he managed to keep all this quiet. He was obviously very determined. Nobody knew a thing about it.'

'Everyone knows now, I take it?' Polly pushed the bank statement and books aside, aware that her sister needed to talk.

'He called a meeting, in the factory, and everyone was there. Some of the older workmen were staggered. However, nobody is going to be fired—Mr Dunn said that the new boss has agreed to keep everybody on, factory, warehouse and office staff. Everyone.'

Polly was frowning. 'So you're not going to be out of a job. Then why so glum?'

'Because...' Maxine paused for effect. This was the worst news. 'Because Dunn & Dunn Limited are being taken over by Grove Langley Limited.' She watched as her sister's eyebrows went up. Was that going to be her only reaction? 'Did you hear me, Polly? I said Grove——'

'Grove Langley. I heard. I must say, it seems a pity.'

'A pity? *Pity?* What they manufacture is junk, junk pure and simple——'

'But they sell a lot of it.'

'Of course they do! It's cheap, dead cheap, cheap and nasty. Those kitchen units they churn out are——'

Her sister interrupted, her eyebrows rising further. 'Dear me, you are upset, aren't you? Is there a snobbish streak in you I've never known about? So what if it is cheap? It's popular, it sells, it'll probably mean more jobs on the estate.'

'Actually, no. Mr Dunn said we could expect few changes. He said Grove Langley intend to keep on the name Dunn & Dunn, to carry on making the traditional furniture.'

'Then what on earth are you going on about? Honestly, Maxine! You come home with a face two feet long, you hit the bottle and let me think you've lost your job—and now you're telling me there aren't going to be any changes. *What* is all the fuss about?'

Maxine couldn't explain; it would sound silly. She glanced around the dining-room; all the furniture in here had been made by Dunn & Dunn and it looked as good now as it had when it had been bought, years ago. It was more than a pity that Grove Langley were taking over, couldn't Polly see that? Grove Langley specialised in kitchen and bedroom units—what did they know about *real* furniture, about craftmanship? Not a thing! If nothing else, the standards would drop.

'You wouldn't understand, Polly. All the staff, without exception, are happy with the way things are now. We like the place. Mr Dunn's workers are content, there's a good atmosphere, there's never a dispute and nobody has ever heard of the word strike. And all the credit for that is his, because a place is only as good as the man who runs it. I've been particularly happy in my job.'

'I know that.' It was because of this that Polly had long since stopped pointing out how wasted Maxine was on the likes of John Dunn with his outdated methods and his old-fashioned ideas.

'And I'm very fond of Mr Dunn.'

'I know that, too. So maybe you'll grow fond of the new boss. When's he taking over?'

'In two weeks, at the beginning of February. Two weeks, for heaven's sake!'

'Have you been told anything about him?'

Maxine shrugged. 'Only his name. It's Kurt Raynor. He's the chairman and managing director of Grove Langley and he's coming in tomorrow to meet our work-force. I'll get to meet him at nine-thirty.'

'*His* work-force.'

'Not yet, it isn't. It sounds hard, doesn't it?'

Polly looked heavenward. 'You've lost me. What sounds hard?'

'That name. Kurt. Kurt Raynor.'

'You're being silly. Look, I have to get ready— David's coming for me at seven.'

If David was coming to collect Polly, it meant they were going into Cheltenham for the evening. Had they been going to Oxford, she would have collected him. David's home, or rather his small bachelor pad, was just this side of Oxford. 'Are you going to the pictures?'

'No. A concert. Then dinner.'

Maxine glanced at the engagement ring on her sister's finger. She had worn one herself a year ago, very briefly...

Getting engaged to Francis Lyon had been a mistake; marrying him would have been the ultimate mistake. They simply hadn't known one another well enough to get engaged; it had all happened so quickly, their thinking they'd fallen in love. Basically they had had nothing in common, nothing at all, and even thinking about that episode was still enough to bring

Maxine out in a sweat. When she thought about how close she had come to——

'Max?'

'Mm?'

'I was saying, I don't like to go out and leave you when you're feeling so down.'

'Oh, I'm going out, too. I have a date.' She glanced at her watch, smiling inwardly as she waited for the inevitable questions. Her dates since Francis had been few and far between.

'With whom? Why didn't you tell me? I take it it's a man?'

The younger girl was laughing now. 'I didn't tell you because I didn't have the chance—you spent all day with David yesterday and I didn't see you, remember?'

'You could have told me this morning.' Polly held up a hand, smiling. 'OK, forget that, I know I'm not the most communicative person first thing in the morning.'

There was also little time to chat in the mornings. Polly was a teacher, an extremely conscientious one, at a school half an hour's drive away, and she left the house at eight every day. Maxine's work was much nearer and she didn't start until nine-thirty, so the two of them only met for a few minutes in the mornings.

'So who is he?' Polly persisted.

'William Harrison. He's twenty-nine, fairly tall, blondish, single and rather nice-looking. He's the new doctor at the Grange End practice.'

'But we don't go to the Grange End practice.'

'No, I met him in church yesterday. Reverend Simmonds introduced us but——'

'And he asked you out, just like that?'

'But, I was going to add, I had in fact already met William. He was called to the orphanage last week— I'm afraid we're in for a flu epidemic there.' Maxine grimaced. There were currently twenty-five children in St Hilda's, the home where she visited and helped out on Saturdays. If they all came down with flu it would be like a circus and William would really have his work cut out.

She checked her watch again. 'Are we going to have a battle for the bathroom?'

Polly shook her head. 'No, I did all that when I got in from school. It's all yours.'

By the time Maxine was soaking in a hot tub she felt better about everything. It was a quarter past seven when she got out of the bathroom. She had to get a move on—William was picking her up at eight and her hair took ages to dry; it was thick, naturally blonde and naturally curly, and it was a pain. It always wanted to do its own thing and she had long since given up trying to tame it. She blew it almost dry and quickly applied a light make-up, just mascara and a touch of eye-shadow to accentuate the blue of her eyes. A dab of lipstick, a dab of perfume and she was ready— except for her clothes. She stepped into a soft, pink woollen dress and struggled for minutes with the long zip at the back. Polly had already left the house, there was no one to help and she was *not* going to ask William to zip her up! On their first date? What sort of impression would that give him?

She finished struggling, successfully, just as the doorbell rang, and hurried downstairs to be greeted by her date—who presented her with a bunch of roses for which he must have paid a fortune. Roses, in January! 'How lovely! Thank you, William. Do come in, I'll just pop these in a vase and get my coat . . .'

It was a super evening. She got home just after midnight and went straight to bed, wishing Polly were home so she could tell her how nice it had been. William Harrison was charming, knowledgeable and humorous, a very good companion.

'Is that all?' her sister asked the next morning. 'I mean, is that all you're telling me?'

'That's all there is to tell.' Maxine was still in her dressing-gown; Polly was about to leave. 'Except that we had a delicious meal.' William had taken her to the Copper Kettle, a cosy, chintzy pub-restaurant where the food was superb, where log fires blazed, where one was so warm and comfortable one could forget it was the depths of winter. 'He didn't make a pass, if that's what you want to know. He is, in every respect, a gentleman.'

'You sound quite taken with him.'

'No. Well, yes. Put it this way, if he rings me, as he said he would, I shan't be sorry.'

'Oh, heck, look at the time! I must go, you can tell me the rest later.'

Maxine smiled and waved. There wasn't any 'rest'. Hadn't Polly believed her? She chuckled as she got to her feet, heading for the stairs. It was time to get dressed.

The local radio station was warning of black ice on the roads. Maxine took note, leaving the house a few minutes earlier because she intended to drive slowly. She did just that—but when she came to a junction in the centre of the village, her car skidded the instant she touched the brake. It was not the best way of starting the day, and it shook her up even though no damage was done. After that she drove even more slowly and got to the office several minutes late, unfortunately.

She spotted the unfamiliar car immediately she turned into the yard where the employees parked. There was bags of room for parking. The factory, the office and the warehouse were in separate buildings, standing in five acres of land, much of which was just grass. Automatically Maxine's eyes went to the window of her boss's office before going back to the sedate black Volvo, an estate model, the newcomer on the car park. So Kurt Raynor was here but Mr Dunn hadn't arrived yet, his car wasn't here.

Quickly she went inside, her head bobbing in greeting as she passed through the general office to get to her own office. One of the typists was in there, waiting for her, looking anxious.

'Maxine, thank goodness!' It was a fierce whisper. 'The new owner's here to see Mr Dunn. He said their appointment was for nine-thirty—but Mr Dunn hasn't turned up yet.'

'I know. Don't worry, Denise. Have you offered Mr Raynor a cup of coffee?' The percolator in the general office was constantly on the go, and everyone helped themselves from it.

'Yes. He didn't want one.'

Maxine shed her coat, hat and scarf. 'Right. Thanks, Denise, I'll go in and have a word with him in a jiff.' She sat down and changed her boots for a pair of shoes before pushing her fingers quickly through her hair in an effort to lift it. The curls had been flattened by the woolly hat—an unflattering thing to wear, but necessary. It was so *cold* at the moment, too cold for snow.

Those were her thoughts as she walked into Mr Dunn's office, unaware that she was frowning. 'Mr Raynor?' He was standing, looking out of the window, his back to her. He was a tall man, broad-shouldered and looking even broader in the heavy sheepskin coat he had on. He turned around slowly, an air of boredom about him.

Maxine had no time in which to school her features, no time in which to think about it. Kurt Raynor was so—so unlike what she had expected him to be! Why had she assumed he would be much older? He was young, only in his thirties, not particularly handsome but certainly attractive in a hard, lean-featured sort of way, with hair the colour of sand and dark brown eyes which... which were looking at her with the utmost disapproval.

'None other.' He did not smile, nor did he offer his hand. 'And you are?'

'Maxine Smith, Mr Dunn's secretary.'

'Smith?'

'Smith.' She smiled, a friendly smile, adding the remark she always added when she was teased about her name. 'I know, there are a lot of us about!'

He still made no move, either to shake her hand or to do anything else. Awkwardly she said, 'Won't you sit down, Mr Raynor? I'm sorry you've been kept waiting.'

'I prefer to stand. What time do you normally start work, Miss Smith?'

'I start at nine-thirty. Mr Dunn—well, I'm sure he'll be along shortly.' Her voice dwindled. Kurt Raynor was looking pointedly at his watch. It occurred to her that it had to be getting on for ten now, and he must be thinking her unpunctual. 'There's a lot of ice on the roads today,' she informed him, probably unnecessarily. 'And this is the first time I've been so late in four years, Mr Raynor. I don't think that's a bad record, do you?'

He just looked at her, saying nothing. Maxine stood in the middle of the office, several feet away from him, but the man's presence, the aura about him which she could not name, seemed to reach out and touch her. It was not a pleasant feeling. His brown eyes were dark, alert and cold, looking at her now as if he expected something of her.

'You're sure you wouldn't like a cup of coffee?' She didn't know whether to go or to stay, to help pass the time by talking to him.

'I'm sure.'

'Then is there anything—anything else I can get you?' Beyond her smile the feeling of awkwardness had increased. Why was she feeling so self-conscious with him? What was keeping Mr Dunn? And why, for heaven's sake, couldn't Kurt Raynor at least bring himself to return her smile?

'What you can do, Miss Smith, is sit down and tell me about yourself. You and I will be working together in the initial stages.'

The initial stages? What did that mean? Stages of what? She glanced at the clutter of papers covering the leather chesterfield settee and opted for the chair facing the desk. John Dunn's office was perpetually cluttered and he would not allow her to tidy it up. He knew where everything was, he had his own system and it worked.

'You—won't be based here permanently then, Mr Raynor?'

'Just as long as it takes to sort things out. I'm on the board of several companies; I move around quite a bit.'

'Then who——?'

'Miss Smith, you were going to tell me about yourself.'

And she had been asking questions instead. Well, she was entitled to know whom she would be working for, working with. Of course she was, but now was not the time to ask. This cold-eyed person was not easy to talk to; he was clearly a man of few words and he seemed to resent her questions. 'Well,' she began, 'I left school with six O levels and three——'

'Not that sort of thing.' He waved a hand impatiently, his car keys jangling from a finger. 'I take it for granted that you're qualified for your job. I want to know about yourself, your life.'

'My life?' she echoed. How was that relevant? She looked at his face, shrugging inwardly and telling herself that he must have his reasons, that this was not idle conversation he was making. 'I'm not sure where to start. Er—I live with my sister——'

'Where?'

'In Oldfield. It's a village ten minutes from here.'

He nodded as if he knew exactly where it was. 'Is your sister younger or older than you? What does she do? And tell me about your parents.'

Maxine looked at him blankly, at a loss. He was leaning against the windowsill now, arms folded across the broad expanse of his chest. His stance was negligent but his expression was one of expectation. What *did* he expect of her? And where should she start? 'My parents—I . . .' She heard herself, sounding idiotic and hesitant, and knew a rush of resentment towards the man. He made her nervous; she wasn't normally like this. 'Mr Raynor, I'll gladly answer your questions, one at a time, though I fail to see the relevance of all this.'

'Relevance to what?'

'To the fact that we'll be working together . . . in the initial stages.'

His brows, which were the exact shade of the sand colour of his hair, rose slightly. 'Are you telling me to mind my own business?'

'Not at all. It's just that I think——'

'You're wasting time.' He was looking at his watch again. 'I'm here today to meet all the employees. You are one of them. Well?'

Was everyone going to get the third degree, then? Maxine didn't ask. Instead she plunged into the details of her life and those of her family. After all, there was nothing highly personal in his questions. She told him about Polly and what she did for a living, that she was two years older than herself and was engaged to David, who was another teacher at the same school. About herself she told him she lived a quiet life and was continuing her education at night school, learning Spanish and improving her French. 'My father and my stepmother, his second wife,' she added, 'live in Brussels. Daddy works for the government. He'll be posted there for at least another year. We all get together two or three times a year, either in Oldfield or in Europe somewhere.' She smiled at the idea, looking at him with enthusiasm in her eyes. 'This year we're getting together at Easter; we're renting a villa in the south of France. I hope that will be all right with you, my taking two weeks off at Easter?'

'Easter? That's a long way off, Miss Smith. We shall have to wait and see what happens, shall we not?'

Maxine didn't respond.

'Go on,' he said. 'Tell me more.'

'More?' She shrugged. 'Well, I think that's about it.'

But it wasn't. The questions started again, one after the other, and they got more and more personal.

'What happened to your mother?'

'She died when I was thirteen.'

'When did your father remarry?'

'When I was in secretarial college—when I was eighteen.'

'And how long ago was that, Miss Smith?'

'I'm twenty-three.'

'And what of your love life? You didn't mention that.'

Maxine stared at him. This question was so unexpected that she had no answer ready. It was her turn to look at her watch now, to break the contact of those cold dark eyes, to play for time while she composed herself. Irritation was making itself felt, very much so. Why was he going into such detail? What made him think he had the right? He couldn't possibly plan to question everyone so closely!

Her voice was stiff when it finally came out. 'No, I certainly didn't. If you intend to ask everyone their life history, you'll need to spend more than the day here.'

To her surprise there was no irritation in his retort, there was just that boredom she had felt when she'd first walked in on him. 'I shan't be working in close proximity with everyone, Miss Smith. You are going to be my secretary. At least, I'm going to give you the opportunity of being my secretary.'

She finally understood. He wanted to know her, about her, and if he didn't like what he learned she might find herself out of a job after all. Well, that was all right by her. Suddenly she didn't give a damn about staying on here, convenience or no convenience, but she was equally curious as to how far this man would go with his audacious questioning. 'I see.' She spoke quietly but audibly, her head coming up in defiance. 'Well, Mr Raynor, what exactly do you want to know?'

'Whether you're on the brink of getting engaged, like your sister.'

'No. I'm not.'

'So for you there are no marriage plans on the horizon? You're not itching to hear the patter of tiny feet?'

'No to both questions.'

'There's no special man in your life?'

'There's no man in my life at all, Mr Raynor, special or otherwise.'

His eyebrows rose again. 'That doesn't sound healthy.'

With that, their eyes met and held. He had questioned her at a deeply personal level when he really must know as well as she did that this was quite out of order. Maybe she should have said as much instead of answering his questions; maybe she shouldn't have allowed her curiosity its rein. 'Nor is it unhealthy. Let's just say I'm between boyfriends, shall we?'

'I can take it that you're strictly a career girl, then?'

'You can take it,' she said crossly, getting to her feet, 'any way you wish to take it. Now please excuse me, I want to make a phone call.' An awful thought had just struck her—maybe Mr Dunn had been taken ill? His heart . . . She turned her back on Kurt Raynor and reached for the phone at the other end of the desk. 'Mr Dunn is not a well man and it's just occurred to me that——'

The sentence wasn't finished before the office door opened and John Dunn breezed in looking pleased with the sight that greeted him, his eyes sparkling, his cheeks pink from the cold. Looking, Maxine thought, as fit as a fiddle. 'Mr Dunn! I was just going to ring you—I thought you might be ill.'

The elderly man patted her on the shoulder, his other hand reaching at the same time to shake that of Kurt Raynor. 'My apologies, Kurt. I witnessed an accident on the way here and I had no choice but to hang around and give a statement to the police. The roads are treacherous. Black ice. Well!' he boomed, giving no one a chance to comment. 'I see you two have met.'

Maxine thought she caught a hint of amusement in the younger man's eyes. Perhaps not—those dark eyes had given nothing away so far. They were watching her now, impassively, and for one wild moment she wanted to protest to her old boss that her would-be boss had been giving her the third degree. Instead she said, 'Yes.'

'Splendid, splendid! Maxine is a good girl, Kurt, an angel, as I'm sure you'll find out for yourself.'

There was no hint of amusement now, fleeting or otherwise. Kurt Raynor merely looked her in the eyes . . . but it was as if he could see her very soul. She recalled only too well the last specific questions he had asked her and there was no way she could prevent her blush when he spoke. 'An angel?' It came drily, quietly, his eyes not leaving hers. 'Well, she certainly sounds too good to be true, from what I've heard . . .'

CHAPTER TWO

'HAVE you quite finished?' Polly was getting impatient. She had been at the dining table again, marking exercise books when Maxine got home.

'No, not quite!' Maxine put both hands flat on the table, her eyes searching for the indignation her sister ought to be feeling. Polly had had a verbatim report of the meeting with her prospective boss and had listened throughout with an irritatingly impassive face. 'Don't you think he had a nerve, Polly, asking me all those personal questions?'

'You needn't have answered them. These days, employers can't discriminate——'

'I know, I know that. It's just——' Maxine broke off, aware that what she was about to say would sound strange. 'It's just that I was . . . sort of fascinated as to how far he would go.'

'Well, if you will insist on being perverse, what have you got to complain about?'

'When I tell you what he did and said next, perhaps you'll understand why I am *not* looking forward to this change-over.'

'So tell me.'

Maxine drew herself erect in her chair, eyes flashing with the annoyance which had not left her all day. 'He looked me up and down, very deliberately mind you, if not suggestively, and said to Mr Dunn that he had omitted to tell him that his "angel" had the face and figure to match.'

'Well?' Polly shrugged expansively. Her deep blue eyes, so like Maxine's, were making no attempt to hide their amusement.

'Well? Is that all you can say?'

'Don't you like compliments?'

'Compliments! Can't you see how sarcastic he was being?'

'Frankly, no.'

'That's because you weren't there. If you'd heard the tone of voice, seen the look on his face...' With an unladylike snort Maxine pushed herself to her feet, recalling only too clearly the way Kurt Raynor had gone on to smile. He had actually smiled for the first time, slowly, almost sensuously, the mouth curving widely to reveal white, even teeth. And in spite of his sarcasm the effect of it on Maxine had been devastating. Mr Dunn had laughed about the angel-face-figure remark and then Kurt Raynor had laughed, too, and everything about him had changed. The dark brown eyes had been suddenly lit, the air of boredom had been chased away and rich, deep laughter had been emanating from him, as if this were all a great joke.

At that point, Maxine had walked out of the room and left them to it.

'I still don't see what you're fussing about,' Polly said. 'If you disliked him so much, why not hand your notice in?'

'That,' came the scathing reply, 'is ridiculous!'

Polly spoke softly, smiling again. 'Why? Because working so close to home is convenient to you?'

'No. Because I feel as if I've been challenged. Because I wouldn't give him the satisfaction, *that's* why. Because I strongly suspect he's expecting me to do just that!' She walked to the doorway, feeling no better for having given vent to her feelings. 'I'm going to make dinner, I have to leave in an hour.'

Polly didn't turn round to look at her sister. She was grinning from ear to ear and she didn't want Maxine to see it. Challenged, she'd said. Good! It was high time Maxine had a challenge in her life. 'You're going to night school, Max?'

'Of course I am, it's Tuesday.'

'But the roads——'

'I'll take it easy, don't worry.' Maxine flounced off to the kitchen. This was one night she was not going to miss evening class—she needed some distraction from the impact Kurt Raynor had had on her.

Impact. It was not too strong a word. He had been on the premises until four o'clock that day. She had seen him crossing the yard with Mr Dunn, going into the factory, the warehouse; she had seen him talking to people in the general office, and only when he had left had she felt at ease again. He had not spoken to her further except to say goodbye, yet she had anticipated all day long another encounter with him.

What she did not anticipate was seeing him again so soon, that very evening. As she left the house for night school, to her knowledge she was not going to see Kurt Raynor again until the first Monday in February, when he took over. Between now and then there was a lot of work to do; Mr Dunn wanted to leave things 'ship-shape', he said. He said also there would be a staff party on the Friday he left, to be held in the general office, and it was with that pleasant thought that she set off in the direction of Cheltenham.

Several hours later she was almost home again, all thoughts of work gone from her mind. She was talking to herself in French as she drove; five minutes more and she would have got home without incident—but that was not to be. As she slowed the car at a T-junction in the lanes approaching Oldfield, it went out of control, the tyres refused to grip the road and she went sailing helplessly across the white line.

'Oh, lord!' Crying out in her mother-tongue, she reacted automatically, swiftly, turning the wheel into the skid as she had been taught. It didn't help—her small car had a life and a mind of its own. How the oncoming vehicle avoided her, she didn't know. To do so, however, its driver had to pull sharply to the right. And still her car kept moving! It was heading towards the bigger vehicle at an alarming rate and all logic, all she had been taught about skidding, fled her thoughts. She stood hard on the brakes.

Miraculously, it proved the right thing to do.

Her car stopped instantly, just inches from the other vehicle. It was a Rolls-Royce, a shape too familiar not to be recognised at once. Already its driver was out, a large figure looming in the darkness. Maxine saw him from the corner of her eye as he approached her window but it was seconds before she looked at him. Her head had dropped on to her hands on the steering-wheel, her entire body was shaking and for the life of her she couldn't move, not for several seconds, not until she had taken some deep breaths.

By this time the man was knocking on the window, shouting at her. 'Are you all right? Are you all right?'

She lifted her head but, before she could answer, her door was wrenched open. 'Why the hell didn't you——? *You!*'

Shock upon shock. Maxine's eyes widened with disbelief as she stared into the eyes of Kurt Raynor. It was too weird, too strange . . . where was he going, where had he been? Why was he driving a different car from the one he'd been in that morning? What was he doing here, so near her home? She had lived in this area all her life and had never, ever seen Kurt Raynor before. Before today, that was.

'Why didn't you answer me?' he demanded. 'I thought you were injured!'

Her eyes closed of their own accord, her voice very small as she spoke. 'N-no. I'm—I'm OK.'

'You're sure?'

She opened her eyes, looking up at the grim features with a shudder. It had been so close...that feeling of being out of control had been awful, one she did not want to experience again. 'I'm sure.' She waited then, waited for an explosion of temper, for the recriminations, accusations.

None came.

Long seconds passed as they looked at one another, saying nothing. It was Maxine who broke the silence. 'I'm—sorry. It was entirely my fault, the ice——' She looked over at the Rolls and shut her eyes. Had there been a collision, she would not have had the protection of a sturdily built car; her own vehicle was by comparison a tin can.

'Get out, Miss Smith.' It was a quiet command.

'Wh-what?'

'I said get out of your car.'

She did, thinking he wanted to see for himself that she was uninjured. Her booted feet planted themselves firmly on the road and she stood; then, at once and without warning, her knees buckled. Long, strong arms caught her, she was pulled tightly against the body of Kurt Raynor and was bombarded with panic, with a dozen impressions in a matter of seconds. There was the scent of him, tangy and masculine in the clear night air, there was the size of him, the sheer bulk of him, clad in the heavy sheepskin he had worn earlier. At his neck she could see a bow-tie, black against the glistening white of his shirt. This was right in front of her eyes, because without her high-heeled shoes he was a head taller than she. Added to all that there was her feeling of foolishness, and then another sensation, one of a shock she could not identify. Almost roughly she put her palms flat on his chest and pushed free of him—or tried to. His big hands moved swiftly to her bent elbows and he lifted her clean off the ground.

'Take it easy!' he barked. 'It's as slippery as hell here, now watch it!' He set her down, easily and slowly, as if lifting her had been merely an exercise for him.

'I'm—all right.' She wanted to protest, to bark back at him, but that was all she could say. She was still trembling badly. 'I'm—is that your car?'

'No, I stole it for a joy-ride, hoping I'd bump into you.'

She clamped her mouth shut, unamused by his retort. 'I take it it's undamaged?'

'It's undamaged.'

That was all she wanted to hear. There was no point in this, their standing around in the middle of the lane in the darkness. Her vehicle was in such a position that other cars would be unable to pass—not that there were any around. 'In that case I'll be on my way.'

'Not so fast.' His hand snaked out and caught her wrist as she reached for her door. With a jerk of his head, he said, 'Get in my car. I'll park this for you and I'll take you home in my car.'

'There is absolutely no need for that.' Indignation rose to the fore. 'I am perfectly capable——'

'You are perfectly capable of killing yourself. And where would that leave me? Looking for a new secretary.'

'Oh, how charming! Now look, Mr Raynor——'

'No, you look. Look at yourself. Your teeth are chattering, your knees are knocking, your face is going blue with cold and your brain has seized up. At least I think it has. Or is this the norm? Are you this stupid around the office? This stubborn? If you are, you're in for a rude awakening. Now get in my car!'

Later, much later, Maxine would ask herself why she obeyed him, but for the moment no such question was in her mind. She was too shocked to think straight, shocked by the near accident and by his outrageous sarcasm. Oh, she had heard that, all right, but she was unable to retaliate. Anger had robbed her of speech, and she was unable to do more than glare at him as she walked carefully across the road to the passenger side of the Rolls-Royce.

The luxury of its seats and the interior went unnoticed. She had eyes for nothing except the man who was climbing into her car, and irrelevantly she registered that he was far too big and bulky for it. He eased it along the icy road, straightening it and parking under a lamp.

A minute later he was sliding behind the wheel of his own car, glancing at her as he put the gear lever into drive. 'Take that look off your face, Miss Smith. Your village is within easy walking distance from here, so you can pick your car up in the morning. Right, now I need directions to your house.'

They got there in no time, the arc of the Rolls' headlights catching on the dining-room windows as Kurt Raynor swung on to the driveway. 'Is there no one in?' He cut the headlights, leaving the engine purring softly.

'What? Oh—it looks as if my sister's gone out.' The double garage was open and empty. 'She must have gone over to David's.'

'Then let's hope she has better luck than you had on the roads tonight. I'll see you indoors.'

'There's no need.' She spoke crisply, opening the passenger door at the same time as he opened his door. She was just beginning to steady inwardly but her hands were still shaking. Privately she was glad to have been driven the last mile home—but there was no way she would let him know it. 'There was no need for any of this, actually, and for the record I'll have you know that I resent your commandeering me.'

'Really?' He was beside her now, disregarding her protest in a tone of utter boredom. 'By the way, must you wear that woolly hat? You do look ridiculous in it.'

To Maxine's horror tears sprang to her eyes. What was wrong with her? Where was the jocular reply she would have given had it come from someone else, some other time? That was it—it wasn't that he had the power to upset her, it was the near miss she'd had in her car. She must be even more shaken than she'd realised. Swiftly she turned her head away, forgetting the ice as she walked quickly up the drive.

'Miss Smith——' They had reached the front door; he had caught up with her but she was determined not to look at him.

'Well, here we are,' she said coldly, 'I'm safe and sound—satisfied?' She pulled off a glove and shoved the key in the lock. 'Goodnight, Mr——'

Instantly, she knew *instantly* that something was wrong. As the front door swung open she could see nothing out of place, nothing at all, yet she knew. The house was too...still. It was too...too what, exactly? She stiffened, her eyes flying now to those of the man beside her.

Kurt Raynor understood at once. His brows came together, eyes narrowed, his head turning slightly as he listened for a sound. He put a finger to his lips, bidding Maxine to stay where she was with the motion of his hand. She couldn't have moved if she'd wanted to; she watched in silent dread as the big man walked stealthily, surprisingly catlike into the hall.

Burglars! How many of them? What if they tackled Kurt Raynor, took him unawares and hit him with something? Her mouth opened and closed again, it was more than she dared to make a noise.

It was he who broke the silence, an eerie silence. Almost gently he spoke her name, her first name. 'Maxine——' He was level with the living-room, his head turning from what he could see. 'They've gone,' he said simply. 'There's no one here, but——'

But someone had been there. Shocked into action, Maxine dashed inside, gasping as she saw the chaos of her living-room. Everything was overturned. Insanely, chairs and sofas, lamps and tables, anything that could be moved had been overturned. Records were strewn around, cushions had been flung into corners. Two plants had been smashed, the soil from the broken pots scattered all over the carpet. In disbelief she took it all in, wondering why they had wreaked such havoc unnecessarily; there was no order, no sense to their searching. Drawers had been pulled out of the writing bureau and tipped up, their contents lying in a heap, even the glass had been shoved off the wooden tops of the coffee-tables. It was madness. There was no cash in the house, nothing highly valuable—at least nothing of value that was easy to move—and so the burglars had wrecked the room. In frustration, probably.

'Maxine, take it easy!' There it was again, that warning. Had she gone pale? She felt fit to pass out. He knew it, too; his arm went around her waist and she slumped against him. He eased her to the floor—there was nothing else on which she could sit—and sat her with her back against the wall. 'Now lean forward, put your head——'

'It's—all right. I'm not going to faint.' It was passing, the ringing in her ears. In a moment she would be fine. It was just the shock . . . the shock . . .

Kurt Raynor looked at her closely, nodded and left the room. He was back with a glass of water immediately. 'Everything seems to be fine in the kitchen, except for the door. That's where they got in—the lock's been smashed. We obviously disturbed them. They must have seen my headlights, heard my car. Maxine? Can you hear me?'

'Yes, I—would you ring the police for me, please?'

The question seemed to come as a relief to him; it told him she was thinking clearly. He made the call and came back to her side. 'I'm going to check upstairs. Don't touch anything.'

She couldn't have touched anything if she'd wanted to; she couldn't move. There was no strength in her legs, they seemed to have turned to rubber. When her prospective boss reappeared she let out a sigh of relief to see him smiling—nothing had been touched upstairs. 'They started in here,' he told her, 'and that's as far as they got.'

'Thank heaven for that!' She looked at him helplessly, wanting to say, thank heaven for you, too. How could she have brought herself to walk into the house without him? But for him she would still be standing petrified on the doorstep.

Where was Polly? She had made no mention of going out tonight. 'My sister . . . I suppose she's with her fiancé . . .'

'She is, there's a note by the kettle saying she's gone to David's. She says she'll be staying the night there.' At Maxine's look of alarm, he smiled. 'Would you like me to ring her, explain what's happened?'

'Yes, please, I'll—no, I'll do it if you'll fetch the phone. It'll be simpler for me to explain.'

Nothing, it proved, was going to be simple tonight. Polly was stunned, asking questions Maxine was ill-equipped to cope with. In the middle of the call the doorbell rang and Kurt Raynor went to answer it. 'Who's answering the door?' Polly wanted to know. 'Who's with you? Are you all right? Oh, Maxine, this is awful. I'll be there as fast as I can, love. Hold on.'

'Don't! I mean don't rush. Be careful, Polly, the roads are in a shocking state.'

So was Maxine. By midnight the worst was over, the police had lingered and asked their questions, made their examinations, taken fingerprints and asked even more questions. Both Maxine and Polly had answered patiently, repeating facts, telling of when they'd left the house, and why, and when they had anticipated coming home.

Mr Raynor didn't escape the police's questions, either. He had told his tale patiently, explaining that he had been out to dinner and had been on his way home when he met Miss Smith. He explained about their near miss on the ice, how he had brought her home and walked in to find chaos. 'I think we disturbed them,' he said. 'I think they bolted out of the back door the instant they saw my headlights. Unfortunately I didn't realise that immediately or I'd have gone after them.'

The older police officer frowned. 'Just as well you didn't, sir, we don't know who we're dealing with.' He glanced around the room in disgust. 'Hoodlums, by the look of it. They're not professional burglars, I can tell you that for nothing, Mr Raynor. It is R-a-y-n-o-r, isn't it? Kurt, you said?'

It was only then that Polly seemed to register who the stranger in the house was. Maxine saw her gape at him suddenly, although she had introduced everyone long since. Polly's eyes flew firstly to those of her fiancé, who had driven her home, and then back to Maxine's. The question in them was unmistakable. This is your new boss? it said. *This?*

Maxine gave a small nod, glancing beneath her lashes at the man who was sprawled in an armchair that seemed too small for him. He had shed his overcoat and she could see, now, how immaculate he looked in formal evening dress. She hadn't really noticed before—nor had she noticed how very attractive he looked. No wonder Polly was staring.

'And your address, Mr Raynor?' The detective sergeant asked the question politely, showing no response to the reply.

'The Manor, Park Lane, Oldfield.'

It was Maxine's turn to stare. The Manor? So it was he who had bought the place? It had been empty for almost a year. She and Polly had speculated as to who would buy it, what type of person; they had speculated that it wouldn't sell at all unless the price was dropped. It had been on the market for an unthinkable sum of money. The Manor was on the outskirts of the village; it was a huge house, far too big for just a couple. So how many children did Kurt Raynor have?

When the police finally left, everyone set to and restored order as best they could. By then Maxine had forgotten her relationship to the man who had helped her. In this time of crisis he had been wonderful, patient and helpful, clearing up the mess without a thought for his expensive clothes. When everything was settled and a second pot of tea had been drained, she remembered herself and her manners. 'Mr Raynor, I want to thank you. You've been extremely kind and I'm very grateful.'

He smiled. 'And that's my cue to leave, I take it?'

'No!' It was Polly who protested, shooting a dark look at her younger sister. 'I mean, not unless you're ready to, of course. I—well, can I offer you a drink before you go? I mean something stronger than tea?'

'Thank you, but no.' He got to his feet, his presence dominating a room which was by no means small. 'I'll bid you goodnight.' His glance took everyone in as he pulled on his coat, lingering finally on Maxine.

'Maxine.' It was Polly again, the impatience in her voice barely suppressed. 'Show Mr Raynor out, won't you?'

'I was just going to.' She had remembered her manners, what was Polly getting so uptight about? She glanced at her prospective boss, a tinge of colour rising in her cheeks as she caught the smile on his face. Was he laughing at her or with her?

At the front door she found out. 'I see your sister likes things to be done properly. Are you like that, Maxine?' The smile was still there. He leaned against the front door, facing her, preventing her from opening it.

Disconcerted, she said, 'I'm not sure what you mean.'

'I mean proper. Would you describe yourself as . . . proper?'

'I—I like to think I'm well-mannered, if that's what you mean.' What was he getting at? What was behind the question, exactly? His eyes were laughing at her now, the dark brown depths lit with amusement. It suited him, she thought reluctantly, he should smile more often—though preferably not at her.

'Tell me, do you regard it as proper to wear a hat in the house? Do you sleep in that thing?'

She gasped, blushing furiously, her hand reaching up to snatch the woolly hat from the back of her head. She had forgotten all about it. 'I had more important things to think about, didn't I?'

'Hey, why so defensive? Have you no sense of humour?'

Of course she had a sense of humour, a good one. It was just different from his, that was all. 'Right now, Mr Raynor, all I want is a good night's sleep.'

'I'm going, I'm going.' He held up his hands, shrugging. He was also laughing—then, before she could stop him, his hands were in her hair, his fingers raking through the thick blonde curls. 'You have fabulous hair, it's very beautiful. If you must hide it, at least try to find something a little more chic.'

His words, his actions, caught Maxine off guard. She stared up at him, too startled to protest as he finger-combed her curls. It was seconds before she realised how intimate this was—or seemed, the way he was doing it. 'Mr Raynor, I really don't think this is necessary!' She stepped away from him, only to find his hands had dropped to her shoulders.

'What's the matter? Was I behaving improperly?'

Impossibly, she thought. That would be a better word. Exasperated, she had to struggle not to snap at him. 'I don't know where you've got this silly notion from.'

'Silly, is it? Have I been getting wrong impressions about you, this morning and again tonight? You see, I'm convinced that you are an old-fashioned type of girl but—why don't we find out for sure?' In one rapid, fluid movement the hands on her shoulders pulled her forward and Kurt Raynor bent his head to kiss her. But he did not kiss her; his mouth stopped short just inches from hers—and then he was really laughing, leaving her stunned, reddening with anger. Or with relief. Or disappointment. She really didn't know which.

'Just as I thought,' he was saying, so highly amused at her expense! 'The prospect was appalling to you. If you could have seen the look on your face...' He swung the door open and was stepping outside before Maxine could even gather her wits. 'Goodnight, angel, see you in a couple of weeks.'

She jerked into action, closing the door with a bang. Let him think what he liked about that, about her, about *anything*! Her hands moved to her temples; the wretched man had given her a headache. He was so confusing... she didn't know where she was with him most of the time...

'Maxine?' It was a chorus from Polly and David. 'You OK?'

She went in to them to say goodnight, unaware of the brightness in her eyes, the flush on her face.

Polly looked suspiciously at her. 'What's up?'

'Him.' A thumb was jerked in the direction of the front door. 'He's obnoxious!'

'Obnoxious?' This from David. 'But—he was charming! He's been kindness itself tonight, Max.'

'Yes, but——'

'But what?' Polly started gathering cups and saucers on to a tray. 'Did he just say something to upset you?'

Had David not been present she might have told her sister what Kurt Raynor had just done . . . almost done. There again, maybe she wouldn't. 'Sort of. No. Well, yes, actually.'

'You always did have a way with words.' Polly was laughing at her. 'And you're a dark horse—you told me all about your earlier meeting with Mr Raynor but you never mentioned that he's young and as handsome as the devil!'

'Oh, really! Don't exaggerate, Polly, he's attractive, maybe, but——' She broke off; she had already admitted too much. Both Polly and David were laughing at her—it seemed to be her night for being laughed at.

'I'm not exaggerating, I thought he was gorgeous. Rugged is the word I'd use.' Polly caught the frown from her fiancé and said no more about Kurt Raynor's looks. 'As for his personality, if you don't think you'll get on with him, leave, hand in your notice now.'

Maxine's family was always telling her she could get a better job but she was *not* going to be pressured into it, not by Polly or by anyone else—most especially Kurt Raynor. 'I don't want to hear any more about handing in my notice.' She glared at her sister warningly, her voice rising. 'I'm well aware I can get a better job, I always have been, but I'm not going to. I don't need to. Working with that man is going to be a challenge, don't you understand that? There's no way I'm going to hand in my notice!'

'All right, Max——'

'I'm also well aware,' she went on, her voice rising even further, 'that there are a lot of changes on the cards. Well, there's nothing Kurt Raynor can throw at me that I won't be up to, you'll see. More to the point, *he'll* see.'

'All right, all right!' Polly held up both hands as if in defence. 'I've got the point, Max. Honestly! He has got under your skin, hasn't he? I shan't mention your leaving again, I promise. Though I doubt you'll stick it for long...' she added deliberately, smiling inwardly—which was enough to send Maxine flouncing off to bed in a huff.

'Well, David, what do you make of that?' Polly looked at her fiancé and laughed as soon as the door had closed behind her sister.

He seemed delighted. 'It's a long time since I've seen her so passionate about something, anything. She's more like the old Max tonight, isn't she?'

'Exactly! And we can thank Mr Raynor for that.'

The sun was streaming through the curtains when the alarm woke Maxine. She closed her eyes against the light; she had slept badly and she was still tired—tired enough to sleep for several more hours if only it were possible. Maybe it was—if she called the office and explained to Mr Dunn what had happened, he would give her the morning off. He was kind like that; he never quibbled when people took time off for a legitimate reason. Opening one eye, she glanced at the clock. It was too early to ring yet. Perhaps she'd just have another half-hour...

Two and a half hours later she woke, panicking. She dashed down to the kitchen, put the kettle on and snatched up the telephone. She needn't have worried. Her boss informed her that he'd already had a call from Kurt Raynor, who had mentioned what had happened the previous night.

'So take the day off,' he was saying against Maxine's protest. 'You must be exhausted, poor girl.'

'No, but thanks for the thought, Mr Dunn. I'm OK. I'll see you at lunchtime.' To take the whole day would be to take a liberty, she felt.

She put the phone down and made tea, reading the note that had been propped against the kettle. 'Your doctor friend rang just as I was leaving the house,' Polly had written, 'with profuse apologies for calling so early. He said he'd get back to you later. Thought this would cheer you up!'

It did. William Harrison was the only good thing that had happened to her this week. Was he calling for another date?

It wasn't quite one o'clock by the time she got to work. Everything was quiet in the general office, because half the staff of Dunn & Dunn went home for lunch. John Dunn was in his office, beckoning her in eagerly when she tapped on his door and stuck her head around it. He was alone, thankfully. It had occurred to her that the new owner might be around again, but he wasn't.

Mr Dunn wanted a blow-by-blow account in Maxine's own words as to the adventures of the previous evening. She went through it all willingly. She was going to miss her old boss; she fetched coffee for them both and sat talking to him until two, which was the end of the generous lunch-break everyone had. 'What are you going to do with yourself, Mr Dunn?'

'When I retire?' He seemed surprised. 'Didn't I mention that I'm thinking of emigrating?'

'Emigrating!' She forgot for the moment that he had a daughter, his only child, in Australia. Maureen was married to an architect, they had two children and they lived in Perth.

'Maureen has been after me for years, you know, to live with them. I must say, it really tempts me now. She and her family have a very good standard of living, a nice lifestyle...' There was a wistfulness in his voice but Maxine wasn't fooled; Mr Dunn was not short of money, and he could have a very nice retirement right here in England. No, it wasn't that; the people in Australia were all that were left of his family and he must miss being with them.

'Not to mention the sunshine.' She smiled at him encouragingly. 'It sounds like a good idea to me.'

'That's just what I've been thinking. I wouldn't mind——' The ringing of the telephone interrupted him. Mr Dunn answered it himself—there was no one on the switchboard right now and a line had been put through to his office, in Maxine's supposed absence.

'Kurt, hello there! No, you're not disturbing me. I was just chatting to Maxine, we do enjoy our little chats... Mm? Yes, she's right here, bright as a button...'

Maxine looked down at the carpet, trying and failing to shut the conversation out. It was business right enough, she gleaned that much as well as the fact that Kurt Raynor had asked after her.

When Mr Dunn hung up he was looking pleased with himself. He patted the receiver. 'A nice man, that. Fair and square. He knows his mind, knows what he wants and goes after it. He'll be very good for Dunn & Dunn, you'll see.' He sighed, looking around his cluttered office. 'Let's face it, this past year I've been slipping and I know it. I'm tired, Maxine, I've let things get out of control, our order books are only half full, I'm behind the times and—and I don't *care*.'

Suddenly he looked tired. Worse, he looked defeated. 'Mr Dunn, don't do yourself down!' Maxine exclaimed. 'Your family, you, built this business from nothing; its reputation is for quality not quantity——'

'Which is fine,' he cut in, 'if the bank balance remains healthy. Times are changing. One has to change with them.'

To Maxine's frustration he seemed content to leave it at that, so she probed, curious about the changes Kurt Raynor might make.

'I don't know what his plans are.' Mr Dunn looked at her in some surprise. 'I really don't. But not to worry, my dear, he isn't going to fire anyone, he's assured me of that.'

'But he seems like such a hard man.' It was another probe and this time Mr Dunn confirmed what she'd said.

'Hard? Certainly he's hard! One needs to be in this day and age. He's a fighter and extremely successful—he's involved with several companies, did you know that?'

'I had gathered——'

'A very busy man. Dynamic is the word.' He smiled ruefully. 'Quite unlike me, eh, Maxine? I'm past caring, I've had my day.'

She got to her feet and picked up the coffee-cups. 'That isn't true,' she said gently. 'Your priorities have changed, that's all. As for having had your day—wait and see what the Australian climate does for you!'

She left the office to the sound of him chuckling. He was such a dear! How he, who was genuinely so, could think Kurt Raynor nice, she did not understand. Nice was not the adjective she would use.

Authoritative, yes. Complex, yes. Unpredictable, yes. Nice, no!

'Maxine?' She had only just settled at her desk when the phone rang a little after two. Pauline O'Connor was on the switchboard and there was a smile in her voice. 'Dr William Harrison on the line. He called earlier...'

'Put him through, please.' Maxine was smiling, giving nothing away to Pauline. There was nothing to give away. 'William? How are you?'

'I'm fine.' His voice was warm, friendly. 'Your sister told me about the burglary—how awful for you! Did they take much?'

'Not a thing. I think we—I—disturbed them. The end result was just a mess, nothing more serious.'

'Still, an awful shock. I—thought it might be nice to go out tonight, take your mind off it?'

'I'd like that.'

'I remembered that your Wednesdays are free. You go to evening class Tuesday and Thursday, don't you?'

'That's right.' It gave her food for thought— William had mentioned he was on call tonight. Had he juggled his duties with a colleague, perhaps, to fit in with her free evening?

'Would it be very boring of me to take you to the Copper Kettle again?'

'Not at all! I really enjoyed it there.'

'That's what I thought.' There was a smile in his voice now. 'Shall we say eight o'clock again? I'll pick you up.'

Maxine liked William Harrison even more by the time they were halfway through their evening. He thought of the little things; he had arrived promptly, as before, this time with a box of chocolates in his hands. He helped her in and out of his car, he opened doors for her, he saw her seated before he sat. Little things. It provoked a thought. Maybe she did like things to be done 'properly'. Maybe she was an old-fashioned girl, though she had never thought of herself as such...

'Maxine?' William was filling her wine glass when her mind drifted. 'I was saying, my steak's excellent. Is yours?'

'Yes. Sorry, I was just thinking——' She stopped in mid-sentence. She had not been about to say she was thinking of Kurt Raynor, of course, she had been about to cover for her lack of attention. Now, however, she was not merely thinking about her new boss, she was actually looking at him because he had just walked through from the bar. On his arm was a tall blonde, dressed in crimson cashmere and looking gorgeous. Maxine had never seen her before, she was another newcomer to the area. So this was Kurt Raynor's wife? She was lovely!

'Maxine? What is the matter?'

'I'm sorry, William.' She moved her eyes swiftly back to her host, away from the attractive couple who were being seated in a corner. Why was she so relieved that the big man had his back to her now? Why did she want him not to have noticed her? And why should he notice her anyway? There was much to hold his attention. 'I just thought I saw someone I knew coming in.'

William was smiling. 'You did. Since you're going to be working for him in a couple of weeks, I presume you have met him.'

Startled, she opened her hands as if in appeal. 'You know Mr Raynor?'

'He was at a dinner I attended last night, a charity do in Oxford.' William turned around to look, making no effort to hide his curiosity. 'He left early, but not before I'd talked to him for a while, about the area, us both being newcomers. I didn't even known Dunn & Dunn was being sold—you never mentioned it on Monday.'

'I didn't think you'd be interested.'

'I'm not particularly.' He smiled again, his eyes shifting to look at the gorgeous blonde, which in turn made Maxine smile.

'His wife is lovely, isn't she?'

William turned his attention back to her. 'Oh, that isn't his wife. He isn't married—I asked him when he told me he'd bought the Manor. I was surprised; it's rather large for a single occupant.'

So Kurt Raynor was a bachelor, Maxine thought; she should have realised the blonde wasn't his wife. Had she been, she would probably have been in the Rolls with him last night. She turned to look at the couple again, speculating. Unable to see Kurt's face, she did have a clear view of the woman looking at him with open admiration, her eyes riveted as if she was unaware that there were other people in the room. She was flirting openly, too, her long slender hands moving expressively as she talked to him.

Maxine turned away, only to see from the corner of her eye a moment later that Kurt Raynor was approaching her table, alone, his hand outstretched to William. 'So, Dr Harrison, we meet again. It was William, was it not?'

William nodded, smiling. 'That's village life for you. The coincidence is not our meeting tonight, but meeting last night in the city.'

'Yes, it's a small world.' The cliché came self-mockingly. 'Well, it's nice to see you again. As for you, Maxine,' he added, finally nodding in her direction, 'I trust you're not out with the good doctor because you're in need of his services after your trauma?'

William answered that, eager to reassure, apparently missing the cynicism in the older man's voice. 'Not only would that be unethical, it would be a terrible blow to my ego! No, no, Maxine and I are friends.'

'Friends?'

'Friends,' she parroted. Damn him, how had he managed to make a single word sound like—like some kind of accusation?

'I see, then I shall leave you to it and return to *my* friend.' With an inclination of his head he departed, moving across the room with the light tread that surprised her all over again.

Neither Maxine nor William said anything about him after he'd gone—gone but not gone. He was still in sight, his broad back was square to her and it kept catching her attention in spite of herself. Time and again her eyes were drawn to him, to the expanse of muscle under the beautifully cut jacket. She even noticed that his hair, otherwise straight, curled at the edges, just above his collar...

'Have I lost you totally now? What's going on?' William wanted to know. 'You're looking daggers at the man!'

'What man?'

He laughed at her. 'I have a feeling you'll be looking for a new job in the not-too-distant. I sensed a certain animosity between you and Kurt. Why so?'

'I have no idea,' she said. And, in truth, she hadn't really. It was just—just there. He just managed, somehow, to rub her the wrong way.

When William dropped her off that evening the house was in darkness again. Though Polly's car was in the garage, which meant she had gone to bed rather than out, Maxine was spooked at the prospect of going indoors. William sensed it. 'I'll see you safely inside, don't worry.'

'It's silly, I know. Polly's upstairs.'

'It isn't silly, it's understandable.' He took her keys from her and opened the front door, bowing her inside. She giggled, as she always did when she'd had a couple of drinks, liking him more by the minute. Whatever it was that was missing was unimportant.

Missing? Where had that idea come from? There was nothing missing, surely? Wasn't William Harrison everything she liked in a man? Too hastily she said, 'Come in, William, I'll make some coffee. Will instant do?'

'Sounds good to me.' He seemed disproportionately pleased by the offer.

She laughed, gesturing for him to go into the living-room. 'It's respectable once more. Make yourself comfortable and I'll join you in a minute.'

It was at that point that the evening began to drag; whereas earlier they had talked non-stop, they now seemed to have little left to say to one another. While they drank their coffee Maxine's eyelids were drooping and she was fighting not to let it show.

'You're tired.' At last William got to his feet, taking her cup and saucer from her and placing it carefully on a side-table. Then he took hold of her hand and pulled her to her feet. 'Come on, lights out and——' And suddenly he was kissing her. It just happened; there was but a one-second pause as she stood, her hand still in his, then his free arm came around her and his mouth covered hers.

Maxine backed off immediately, freeing herself with unnecessary force. 'William, please!'

'I'm sorry.' He was clearly taken aback by her vehemence. 'I didn't mean to offend you, Maxine...'

'I'm—you didn't.' She was feeling foolish now. 'I just—you just took me by surprise, that's all.'

He smiled, a mixture of ruefulness and curiosity, and said goodnight. 'I'll see myself to the door. And I'll be in touch, all right?'

'I—yes. Yes, do.' She stayed where she was, wondering why she had just encouraged him to contact her again when in fact she was by no means sure she wanted another date with him. He was nice, very nice, but—there was something not right, somewhere.

CHAPTER THREE

THERE was a shock in store for Maxine the day she began work for Kurt Raynor. With the passing of time she had calmed down by then, had told herself she really must keep an open mind as far as he was concerned. After all, he really had been kind on the night of the burglary. It was just his sarcasm . . .

Since seeing him then she had been extremely busy tying up loose ends for her old boss, and there had been the farewell party. It had been both a happy and a sad occasion, the closing of a very long chapter in John Dunn's life.

It was snowing now, it was eight-thirty on Monday morning and she was standing by her bedroom window, looking at it. There were several inches already on the ground and, if the sky was anything to go by, there was plenty more to come. She glanced at her watch. There was no way she was going to be late today but there was still time to tidy up and make the beds. She had got up earlier than usual, had taken care with her make-up; she had tied her unruly curls in a tight knot on her crown and had opted for the severest, warmest dress she possessed, a black sweater-dress with a turtle neck.

It wasn't until she stepped outside that she realised the snow was even thicker than she'd thought. Thanks to that she arrived at the office precisely at nine-thirty rather than being ten minutes early, as she had planned. Still, her new employer could hardly complain about that. Punctual was punctual.

There was no Rolls-Royce in the car park; she spotted the black Volvo he had used the day she had met him, together with two alien vans and several cars she hadn't seen before. The moment she stepped into the general office, she realised there were workmen on the premises; the banging and clanging on the floor above was deafening. What were they doing? There was nothing on the floor above—the office block consisted of two storeys but all the offices were on the ground floor.

She looked around, frowning. Telephones were ringing, typewriters were clacking, the atmosphere of the general office was quite different. Nobody stopped her for a chat as she passed through, everyone seemed to be subdued, saying no more than 'good morning'. There was tension in the air and it communicated itself immediately. She headed for the ladies' room at the back of the building, suddenly needing to check her appearance in a mirror, to reassure herself that there was nothing about it Kurt Raynor could criticise.

Satisfied, she made her way to her office only to be met with another surprise—it was a spacious room and in one corner was a new desk—why? There was nothing on it, not a scrap of paper or a pen, nothing. She shrugged and hung up her coat, exchanging her boots for the shoes she kept in the office—and she hadn't even had time to put her bag in her own desk drawer before her phone rang. Or rather the buzzer went, which meant it was the boss who wanted her. She picked up the receiver, glancing at the wall which separated their offices as if she would be able to see through it and gauge the mood of the man.

Kurt Raynor was shouting above the noise from overhead. 'So you've finally turned up! Come into my office.'

'I——' He'd hung up! Maxine glared at the wall in amazement, wondering what was the matter with him. What kind of greeting was that?

'Come!' He was sifting through a stack of papers when she went in, not bothering to look at her. 'Sit down, Miss Smith.'

Miss Smith. So it was back to that? Of course it was, this was business. She sat, crossing one leg neatly over the other, her back straight, notepad and pencil at the ready. With as much sweetness as she could muster, she said, 'Good morning, Mr Raynor.'

He answered with a grunt; he still wasn't looking at her and she knew he was doing it deliberately, letting her wait in an uncomfortable silence until he saw fit to talk to her. Minutes passed before he found what he was looking for, then a piece of paper was thrust at her across the expanse of desk which separated them. 'Take a look at this and tell me what's wrong with it.'

Maxine took the paper, which was the carbon copy of an invoice, and saw at once that the prices on it were wrong—to Dunn & Dunn's detriment. 'These customers have been undercharged. Did it—had it gone unnoticed?'

'Unnoticed?' There was a cynical twist to his mouth. 'I personally took a phone call from the customer's accounts department earlier. Honest of them, was it not?' He didn't give her time to answer. 'Yes, it had gone unnoticed. That and how many others, I wonder?'

'Mr Raynor, I have nothing to do with invoicing or——'

'I'm aware of that,' he cut in. He was looking straight at her now, eye to eye, and there was absolutely nothing about his surveillance which acknowledged she was a woman. It seemed that, now he was parked behind Mr Dunn's desk, Kurt Raynor was a totally different man. Different, again.

'I am pointing this incident out to you,' he went on, 'so that you might begin to realise how unbelievably inefficient this company is. I have been here since six-thirty this morning and what I have discovered thus far both horrifies and astonishes me. Suffice it to say there are going to be a lot of changes around here, Miss Smith, and I,' he paused, assessing her, 'am going to need you more than I thought I would. You've been here for four years and you know the running of the business well—if John Dunn is to be believed.'

Maxine's reactions were mixed. Believed? Of course Mr Dunn was to be believed! But ... what a surprise, Kurt Raynor saying he was going to need her more than he'd thought. Should she be flattered? 'I'm at your service, Mr Raynor.'

'Indeed you are, and you yourself are going to make some changes.'

'Am I? Well, if you feel——' She was stopped by the sound of an almighty crash from upstairs and she looked up, half expecting something or someone to drop through the ceiling. 'What's going on up there?'

'Our new offices.'

'New offices?'

'That's what I said. This lot,' he added, with the sweep of an arm that referred to the entire ground floor, 'is going to be converted into a showroom.'

'A showroom?'

'For our wares,' he added facetiously. 'You know, the furniture we manufacture? So it can be displayed in a proper setting. So that buyers can come in and walk around. A *showroom*.' He waited for a retort but Maxine did not make one. He wasn't going to rattle her, no way would she allow that. In any case, his anger wasn't directed at her personally but at the organisation—or lack of it, as he saw it.

'Right,' he went on, 'since you've managed to grasp that much, I'll continue. Our offices, general and individual, will be moved upstairs, into the space which has hitherto been wasted. There will be a new telephone and intercom system and all the manual typewriters will be thrown out in the rubbish and replaced with electronic ones or, in some cases, word processors. Wages will cease to be paid weekly, salaries will be paid monthly and it's with regard to that, among other things, that I want to talk to you.'

He didn't give her a chance to comment; he didn't even pause for breath. 'I've told you I need you for obvious reasons, at least until I've got things sorted out properly, but if you're not prepared to work full time you are of no use to me at all. This is one of the changes you must make. I'm not interested in keeping on a part-time personal assistant.'

'Just a minute!' Maxine's hand shot up, her head moving from side to side in confusion. 'You've just promoted me from secretary to PA and at the same time——'

'At the same time I have indicated that my proposal is contingent upon several things, firstly that your hours will no longer be from nine-thirty till five with an hour and a half's break for lunch. For heaven's sake!'

'Then what will they be?'

'I want you at your desk at nine sharp in future, forty-five minutes for lunch.'

'I see,' she said quietly. 'And when would you have me finish?'

'When the day's work is finished.'

'I see,' she repeated, pausing to count silently to ten. He was getting to her. She hadn't been with him for five minutes and already he was getting to her. 'And my pay rise for the extra hours?'

'There will be no pay rise.' He looked at her as if she'd said something ridiculous. 'Not until you prove yourself. And another thing, you'll be missing your "little chats" over cups of coffee in the future.'

Maxine's mouth clamped together. She could walk out now, right now, without a backward glance, without any regrets. Her feet were almost twitching, wanting to do just that, but she was damned if she would! Her head lifted as she held his gaze; he was waiting, just waiting for her to quit! Inwardly she was seething—his reference to her as a part-timer had rankled and then some. Maybe she hadn't worked long hours before, but she had worked damned hard nevertheless. Softly she said, 'Go on, Mr Raynor, I'm listening.'

There was a slight lift to his brows, much to Maxine's satisfaction. Had he thought he would frighten her off? 'For the moment, that's all. We'll talk again in a couple of weeks—if you're still around. In the meantime you can get cracking with the routine stuff; there's a heap of letters here——'

'Just a moment, Mr Raynor. I haven't yet accepted your new terms of employment.'

'What?'

This time his brows had positively shot up and Maxine smiled inwardly. He had admitted he needed her, she was aware of the strength of her position— but she was going to be reasonable about things. She said as much, adding, 'Since I am, for the moment, an unknown quantity to you. So I will agree to the longer hours you want, but when my new contract of employment is drawn up——'

'Contract?'

'Yes, Mr Raynor. When my new contract of employment is drawn up, it will state that my finishing time is five-thirty—though, as I've already implied, I won't hold you to that. At least, not always.' She added the last sentence with her sweetest smile, noting with further satisfaction that it was he who looked rattled. 'Furthermore, I want a salary revision in one month's time——'

'Three,' he interrupted. 'That'll give me time to assess——'

'One.'

He looked at her crossly but she ignored it. 'Two.'

'Done,' she said.

There was a brief silence during which he continued to survey her. 'I'll have words with Personnel. In the meantime,' he added, pushing three cassettes in her direction, 'you can get on with these letters. I trust you know how to use a dictaphone?'

'Of course. But we haven't got one. Mr Dunn always dictated his letters to me.'

'Look in the top drawer of your desk, Miss Smith.'

'Does this mean I won't be using my shorthand any more?'

'No, it doesn't. I would have dictated to you myself if you'd been here when I needed you.'

Maxine got to her feet, fuming inwardly. Was he always going to be so sarcastic? 'I'm not a mind-reader, Mr Raynor. If you had let me know, I could have been here at nine today.'

'I needed you at six-thirty this morning,' she was informed. 'But that would have been asking too much,

I suppose.' This was added with a smile, one which Maxine could not bring herself to return.

'Far too much. I don't think——'

There was the briefest knock at the door, it opened before Kurt could respond to it—and in walked a stranger. It was a tall, slight, dark-haired, smiling man aged around forty. His shirt sleeves were rolled up, his tie was loose at his neck and there was dust on his shoulders—sawdust.

'Ah, Jim . . . how's it going up there?'

'It's going well, as long as I'm keeping an eye on them.'

'Good. Now meet your new secretary.'

The man's hand was extended before Maxine registered Kurt's words. 'James Ferguson,' he said, with the trace of a Scottish accent.

'Maxine Smith.' She smiled at him; here was a very different kettle of fish—there was nothing ruthless about this man's looks, nothing hard in his manner. She turned to Kurt. 'Did I hear you say I'm to be Mr Ferguson's secretary, Mr Raynor?'

'You did.' He was on his feet now, moving round his desk to stand close by her, towering over her.

Disconcerted far more by his nearness than by what was being said, Maxine had to stop herself from moving away from him. 'But I thought——'

'You'll be working for both of us. Mr Ferguson is one of your new directors, he'll take over as managing director in time. Until then you'll have the pleasure of helping us both. What's the matter—don't you think you'll be able to cope?'

Her smile was pure sweetness and light. She would not, would *not* allow him to get the better of her. No matter what, she would show him what she was made of! 'Of course I'll be able to cope, Mr Raynor.' She turned to James. 'I look forward to working with you.'

The grunt from the big man was satisfying to her; let him spring all the surprises he liked. No sooner had she had the thought than he sprang another.

'Oh, by the way, Mr Ferguson will be working in your office until we're organised upstairs. But you won't mind that, will you, Miss Smith? Such wasted space ... one could hold a dinner-dance in the room next door ...'

'I hate him!' Maxine told her sister. She said the words with vehemence—it was Thursday night and she had got home from work exhausted. She couldn't manage evening class; firstly she didn't have the energy and secondly she would have to rush like mad to make it. Kurt had kept her at her desk until six fifteen.

'You're beginning to sound like a broken record.' Polly was at the stove, putting a cottage pie to brown under the grill. It was her night to make dinner—thank heavens. 'There's no point in keeping on telling me you hate him. You've said it every night this week and you know what the solution is.'

'*Don't!*' Maxine snapped at her. All day and every day she had to hold her temper in check at work—at home, at least, she could give vent to it. The last thing she needed right now was Polly's stock answer to the problem. 'You promised not to say that again—but you keep on saying it! Can't you see it's a matter of pride? I *won't* quit the job; I will not let Kurt Raynor beat me. You know, you've been acting oddly this past week, Polly. I can't seem to communicate with you any more. I'm not the one who's talking like a broken record, you are! Leave, quit, give up. Is that all you can suggest?'

Her sister turned to smile at her. Her mouth opened and closed again until, very quietly, she said, 'Actually, no. I suggest you lay the table so we can eat.'

A week later, on the following Thursday evening, they were having a very similar conversation. Again Maxine was too tired to go to night school, again Kurt Raynor had kept her late at the office. And, again, Polly was urging her to give up, to look for another job.

'You're wasting your breath.'

'OK. I shan't say it again, and this time I really mean it.' Polly was beaming, seeming delighted for some reason. 'Actually, I've been testing you in a way.'

'What are you talking about?' The younger girl pushed her plate to one side. She was having trouble keeping her eyes open.

'Well, I'm not sure how to put this but... I like what's happened to you. I don't want you to leave your job, because these days you're obviously getting the stimulus you need.'

'*Stimulus?* Is that what you call it?'

'Oh, I know you're tired and you feel overworked, but you'll adjust to that soon enough, you'll get used to the new routine. On the other hand—and this is the good news—you're different. You're more positive, more alive.'

'You must be joking——'

Polly shook her head. 'I'm not joking. You're more—animated.'

'You mean angry.'

'Maybe, maybe. But it's not a bad thing, it really isn't. Honestly, Max, I never said anything before, but I worried about you. After breaking off your engagement with Francis, you slipped into—well, a very humdrum existence. Nothing seemed to excite you, to move you, to anger you even. Do you see what I mean? Granted, you did start accepting dates again eventually, but you're more vibrant these days, you're much more like your old self. The reason for it might not be an ideal one but, all things considered, I think Kurt Raynor is good for you.'

She went out an hour later, leaving Maxine alone with her teeming thoughts, her frustrations. More like her old self? What had Polly meant by that? On reflection, she decided Polly was probably right. It was true that she had hibernated for a while after her engagement to Francis had been broken, but...but she'd had no idea that her sister had actually worried about her. Was she different now? If so, it had nothing at all to do with Kurt Raynor. Furthermore, she could *not* agree that Kurt Raynor was good for her!

At a little before ten she went to bed; an early night was in order. She had worked for that man for almost two weeks, only two weeks, and in that time everything had been madness. She could say one thing for him—when he made changes, he made changes, and he made them quickly and efficiently. The partitioning into offices on the upper floor was finished. It had been cleverly worked out—too cleverly. Maxine's office was now in between that of James and that of Kurt, and what she did not like, among many other things, was the glass partitioning that started at shoulder-height. It meant that if one were seated, one could not see from one office into the next, *but*, if one were standing, one could. And Kurt did, often. Several times she had looked up from her desk and caught him watching her, checking up on her, the dark brown eyes brooding. The wretched man must be under the impression she didn't have enough to do! It made her furious.

She turned over in bed and thumped her pillow, wishing she could get thoughts of her employer out of her mind. If the time came when she actually lost her temper, it would be the end. She was like a time-bomb, ticking away slowly. But she wouldn't explode, because things would not go on as they were. These two weeks had been difficult, but now the banging had stopped, all the decorating was finished and all the workmen gone. Given that it had been business as usual while everything was in chaos, it could only get better now, couldn't it? Surely things would settle down . . . ?

But would she, personally, settle down? There was one source of tension which was unlikely to go away—unless and until Kurt absented himself from Dunn & Dunn. Whenever he was near her she felt a different kind of tension, the kind she could no longer ignore even while she despised herself for it. He was not even her type; he was the last man on earth she would want to feel physically responsive to—and yet she did.

Around eleven the following morning, she slipped downstairs to the ladies' room at the rear of the ground floor. These rooms were the only ones not to have been changed in any way, except for a new coat of paint. She heard someone crying before she had even got through the door. It was Mrs Morgan, the wages clerk; she was standing by a basin, splashing cold water on her face and crying at the same time. 'Mrs Morgan! What on earth——'

'I'm leaving!' It all came out in a rush. 'I haven't got anything against the big boss personally, but I *don't* like his methods! I've just given him my notice.'

Maxine sighed. The woman wasn't alone—two of the typists had handed in their notice, too, because Kurt Raynor had informed them they would be working on word processors from the start of next month. In the meantime they had been promised— although they saw it as a threat—a one-week training course in Oxford. 'Mrs Morgan, why? Why don't you take time to let things settle down?'

'Settle down?' She was indignant. 'Maxine, I'm too old to change. Mr Raynor had me in his office this morning and he informed me, cool as you please, that the wages system is to be changed. 'We're all to be paid monthly from next month onwards and—and he's going to get a *computer*!'

Maxine smiled. Mrs Morgan used the word computer as if she were saying something dirty. 'But you're not too old to learn—— '

'Oh, Maxine! I've no desire to, love! I'm due to retire in two years. Do you think I'm interested in learning this new-fangled machinery?'

New-fangled machinery. To her, that was what a computer was. There was no denying that Dunn & Dunn were behind the times, but that was the charm of the place—or had been. Maxine went back upstairs with a heavy heart, wondering how long, in honesty, she would be able to stick it out here. Was her pride worth the aggro?'

James Ferguson was in her office, waiting for her. 'Why so glum?' He was perched on her desk, with more work for her in his hands.

She lowered herself into her chair; if she remained standing she could be seen by the man in the next office—the big boss. It was funny how the new directors had been labelled by all the work-force. The boss and the big boss. Well, the sooner the big boss went about his other business, the better.

As if reading her thoughts, Jim Ferguson said, 'Kurt's gone out, Maxine—he's gone over to Grove

Langley. He'll be in Watford for the rest of the day, so why don't you tell me what's up?'

She hesitated only for a second before plunging in; two weeks with James had shown her that he was neither unapproachable nor unreasonable. 'Mrs Morgan was in the Ladies', crying her eyes out. She's handed in her notice because——'

'I know about it. She'll still get her pension, you know.'

'That isn't the point.'

'Then what is?'

'She's been working for this company for seventeen years.'

'No,' he said reasonably. 'Not this company, Maxine. She's been working for Dunn & Dunn, but not for this company.'

That was true but... 'But it's hard. Mr Raynor's hard. He's come in here like a new broom, changing everything...'

'Listen.' Jim's voice was kind yet firm. 'Nobody has been asked to leave—nobody. Things are changing—they need to, badly—and those people who are not prepared to change with the times, well, it's their look-out. They have a choice.'

'Some choice.' The words were out before she could stop them.

'Look, Kurt is not running an old folks' home here, you know. He has a fantastic business head and he knows precisely what he's doing. Stay around, Maxine—at least, I hope you will—and you'll see, you'll see him triple the business we're doing now in a matter of months. There'll be *more* work for people in the long run. Have you talked to any of the men in the factory lately?'

She hadn't had the chance, she had been so busy. 'No. Nor the men in the warehouse.'

'Then do. It's a different story over there—they're all singing Kurt's praises.'

It was the respect, the near reverence in his voice that brought her head up. 'How long have you known him, Jim?'

He smiled. 'Now, let me see... I first met him when I was twenty, so, almost twenty-one years. I haven't actually known him all that time—I mean, there were several years when I never saw him.'

'Then he—he was still a teenager when you first met him?'

There was only a nod, he didn't volunteer anything except, 'That's right, he was fifteen.'

'Then how come you ended up working together?'

'He offered me a job when he got Grove Langley on its feet; he was twenty-five by then. I hadn't seen him for several years, and he contacted me out of the blue and offered me a job. We've gone from strength to strength together ever since. He made me a director of Grove Langley, and now of this company, and I have a lot to be grateful to him for. He's much cleverer than I. Administration is my strong point, I'm a good manager but—well, it's Kurt who brings in the business. And without the business there wouldn't be anything to administrate, would there?'

'No.'

'So cheer up. Trust him. He knows what he's doing.'

The phone rang before anything more could be said. 'It's for you.' Maxine handed him the receiver. 'It's the headmaster of a school whose name I didn't quite catch.'

A few minutes later Jim was on his way to collect one of his children from school. His third and youngest child had had a bad fall in the playground, so they were sending him home for the day.

'Isn't your wife at home?' Maxine looked at him anxiously. 'There's so much stuff needing your signature, Jim. Will you be back later?'

'Yes, when my wife gets home. She's gone to London for the day, shopping.' He grinned, gave her a quick wave and left.

At two fifteen the big boss rang. A woman who announced herself in a snuffly voice as Linda Storton, Mr Raynor's secretary at Grove Langley, put him through to Maxine.

There was no preamble. 'Put me through to Jim, Miss Smith.'

She stiffened at the sound of his voice; she had come to detest the way he called her 'Miss Smith'. Every time he said it, with that odd inflexion, he seemed to be mocking her. 'I'm afraid he's had to go out.' She explained what had happened, her own voice neutral as she asked if there was anything she could do.

His answer to that was a drawl. 'I'm sure there's a great deal you could do for me—but not in this particular instance. Have Jim call me immediately he gets back, and, by the way, stick around this evening. I'll be back there around six-thirty and I want to talk to you.'

No! she thought angrily. It was Friday, she had a date, and he expected her to wait around till six-thirty because he wanted to talk to her? There were limits. 'No can do, Mr Raynor, I have an engagement tonight. I'm ever so sorry,' she added in a saccharine voice.

'An engagement, eh? You mean you've got a date with your doctor friend.'

'Yes, I mean I've got a date with my doctor friend.' Friend. Why did he have to say it like that?

'And what is he planning to do with you?'

Maxine closed her eyes, counting to three before answering. 'He's taking me to a party.'

'Oh, well, that's all right, then.' It came as quick as a flash. 'Parties never start before nine, that'll give you plenty of time to make yourself beautiful. See you at six-thirty.'

'Mr Raynor——' The line was buzzing; he'd hung up on her! Fuming, she stared at the telephone as if it had bitten her.

'No,' she said aloud. 'No, no, no, no, no!' She would *not* stick around until six-thirty tonight.'

Nor did she; she left the office at precisely five-thirty. The trouble was that she was shaking as she drove home—that was the effect Kurt Raynor had had on her.

She'd had to take a stand. If she gave in to every one of his demands he would use her as a doormat. He was working her like a slave already and paying her no extra for it—which was, of course, her own fault for agreeing to it.

Polly wouldn't be home when she got in, so there would be no one to grumble to; she and David had gone away for the weekend, straight from work. Lucky them. The snow was still hanging around, although the roads were completely clear of it now. Maxine put her car in the double garage and closed the doors. No more driving for her tonight in any case. William was collecting her at eight-thirty; the party was several miles away and he wanted to arrive around nine. Of course Kurt had been right, parties never started earlier. She could have hung around at the office, had she been so inclined, and still have had plenty of time to get ready for William. But why should she?

A long soak in a hot bubble-bath helped soothe her. She dried herself vigorously, slipped into her dressing-gown and was finishing her make-up when the doorbell rang. The clock on the bedside table said a quarter to seven. It would be the milkman. She pottered downstairs and picked up from the hall table the milk money that Polly put there every Friday morning.

But it wasn't the milkman.

Kurt stood on her doorstep, unsmiling, looking bored, just as he had the first time she had ever set eyes on him. 'Naughty, Maxine,' he said. 'Naughty, naughty, naughty!'

CHAPTER FOUR

'I—FOR heaven's sake, come inside!' The rush of cold air made Maxine shiver and she was not going to talk to Kurt Raynor on the doorstep—the neighbours opposite would just love that sort of show. She swung the door wide, closed it after him swiftly and tightened the belt on her dressing-gown. It was satin, a heavy material, perfectly respectable but not exactly the garb she would have chosen to be in for this unexpected visit.

Her employer had walked ahead of her; he was already throwing his overcoat across the sofa when she caught up with him. He was already making himself comfortable in an armchair by the time she invited him to sit down. 'Is there still no news from the police?' he asked. 'About the burglary?'

'Nothing. And I'm quite sure you didn't come here just to ask me that. So, what can I do for you?' Maxine busied herself switching on lamps then stood, arms folded, in the centre of the room. She was all business, determined to ignore the fact that he looked tired—tired but extremely attractive, none the less. His dark eyes had an added mystery in the light of the lamps; the planes of his face had taken on a different look, too, a softer look. 'Mr Raynor? I said——'

'Kurt. Why don't you make it Kurt when we're off duty?'

'I am not off duty—evidently. You wanted to talk to me and you're here in spite of what I told you.'

'Ah, yes, your date with the doctor.' He leaned back, letting his head rest against the wing of the chair, stretching his impossibly long legs out in front of him.

Patiently, she waited. It was all different, again. He was looking at her as if she was a woman, again. Her head came up, her stance aggressive as she withstood the lingering scrutiny of his eyes along the length of her body. But he wasn't going to ruffle her, she was getting used to his tactics.

'Where's Polly?'

'What's that got to do with anything?'

He was still drinking in the sight of her. 'Can I take it we're alone in the house?'

'We are. But don't let that worry you—you won't be here long and you're perfectly safe.'

His bark of laughter, so sudden, so loud, made her jump. She clamped her lips together, wishing she hadn't tried to be clever.

'Do sit down, Maxine, you're making it very difficult for me to concentrate.'

'I happen to be busy, Mr Raynor. I happen to have a date tonight.'

'Very well.' He hooked his right leg over the arm of the chair, shrugging. 'But I think it's only fair to tell you that I can see every contour of what looks like a delicious body through that gown you're wearing. That light behind you is most revealing...'

Maxine moved clumsily, rapidly, to the settee. It was no use, there was going to be a show-down after all, and sooner than she had anticipated it might be. She couldn't carry on with him; she might as well quit right now. She waited until his fresh bout of laughter subsided before tackling him. 'All right, Mr Raynor, you've had your fun and you've won. For some obscure reason you took a strong dislike to me the

moment we met. Why, I can't imagine. You've pre-
tended to give me a chance because you promised John
Dunn you wouldn't fire anyone. Well, you don't need
to fire me, I quit. Now, are you satisfied?'

He picked up on only one word, his sand-coloured
brows rising almost to his hairline. More mockery.
'Dislike? Why, Maxine! I don't dislike you. On the
contrary, you are very refreshing. More so, in fact,
than a good, strong cup of tea. Speaking of which,
are you going to offer me one?'

She couldn't believe it. He wasn't real, surely?
'Didn't you hear me? I said I'm no longer in your
employ—so please leave!'

'OK.' He shoved himself to his feet. 'I'll make the
tea, then.'

And he did. She heard him rooting around in the
kitchen. She stayed where she was, breathing deeply;
she didn't even get up to answer the doorbell when it
rang.

'Maxine? Milkman. He says you owe him two
weeks, he says no one was home when he called last
Friday.'

She glared at him, forcing herself to get up. 'Thank
you, Mr Raynor.'

'Kurt. Make it Kurt. Especially while I'm playing
butler.'

The milkman gave her a very peculiar look; from
where he stood he could see Maxine's unwanted guest
moving around in the kitchen, in his shirt-sleeves now,
and she of course was wearing nothing more than a
dressing-gown! 'I see you've got company. Polly's out
then, is she?' he wanted to know. 'A lovely girl, your
sister...'

'Yes, she's lovely, goodnight.' Maxine almost shut
the door in his face. She was shaking with anger,

wondering what the devil she was going to do; her erstwhile boss was carrying a tray from the kitchen to the living-room just as if he did this for her daily.

'Tea's up!'

'Mr Raynor——'

'Make it Kurt.'

She did. 'Go to hell! Is that curt enough for you?'

He gave her an exaggerated sigh. 'Can you imagine how many times people have made that same joke about my name? I mean, it has its problems and you should sympathise instead of mocking. What's it like for you when you book into a hotel using the name Smith?'

Laughter bubbled inside her, laughter at herself as much as him. When would she learn? She wouldn't win, not with him! He was taking no notice of her whatever, she might just as well give in gracefully and hear him out—but she wasn't going to laugh out loud. Resignedly she sat. 'All right. So be it. You wanted to talk to me, so I'll listen—and I'll pour the tea.' She was leaning over to do just that when the satin of her gown parted and gave him a perfect view of her breast. She glanced at him, hoping he hadn't noticed, tugging the material back into place.

He'd noticed all right. He wasn't smiling now, nor was there any more sarcasm or unwelcome wit. 'Maxine,' he said, in a voice far softer than anything she'd heard before, 'please do me a favour, and no arguments this time. Run upstairs and put some clothes on.'

She obeyed without a word, wondering why he seemed annoyed. Any other man ... but Kurt Raynor was not any other man.

'That's better.' He looked her over as she came back into the room, dressed in the denims and chunky sweater she had pulled on. She registered at once that she was walking into a different atmosphere; there was a peculiar stillness in the air and he was still talking in that soft voice.

'Where is your sister?'

'She's gone away for the weekend.'

'And what are your plans?''

'You know my plans.'

'Only as far as tonight's concerned. Is—William Harrison spending the weekend here with you?'

'Certainly not!' The words burst from her without thought, without hesitation. 'I hardly know the man!' If she had known the man she was talking to better, she'd have known whether or not he was suppressing laughter. As it was she couldn't be sure.

He cleared his throat. 'Oh. Well, excuse me, I didn't mean to offend your... sense of propriety.'

'Oh, really! You just can't resist, can you? If you're not being sarcastic, you're sending me up. What is it with you? What have I done to upset you?' She was on her feet, shouting now. Damn the man, was he incapable of holding a sensible conversation? 'Look, Mr—Kurt, if you want to talk to me, talk to me. I don't think I can stand your company much longer; you're making me into a nervous wreck!'

'Then relax,' he shrugged. 'Sit down. Drink your tea.'

'Just leave, will you? *Go!* I've changed my mind, I'm not willing to listen any more.'

When, later, Maxine tried to recall what happened next, she could not. It all happened so fast. Kurt Raynor was suddenly on his feet and both her wrists were pulled behind her back, held in one of his hands.

'Maxine, stop this!' he was booming. 'I am rapidly losing patience with you, I've never met such a stubborn, aggressive, paranoid——'

'Paranoid? *Paranoid!* Will you let go of me?' She wrenched her body so hard that she toppled sideways. He let go of her and caught her at the same time, his arms clamping around her to stop her falling.

In a split second all was silent and still again. In a split second the atmosphere changed again. Maxine was hard up against him, feeling the rub of her breasts against the broad wall of his chest. Their eyes had locked. Neither of them moved a muscle. There was only the sound of their breathing, only the touch of body against body to tell her she wasn't dreaming this. No, she wasn't dreaming, yet it was in a dreamlike manner that she raised her face, very slowly, knowing he was going to kiss her and meeting him halfway, wanting it with a depth of feeling that shook her.

But she was wrong. He did not kiss her. He broke the silence, the stillness, by putting her from him and stepping back, turning away from her as he spoke. Quietly he said, 'Please sit down. Let's pretend I've just walked in here and start again.'

It was seconds before she could find her voice—disappointment was choking it off. It didn't make sense. He didn't make sense. She had been so sure he would kiss her this time, had been sure that he wanted it as much as she. She didn't understand the man, she never had and it seemed she never would; he was never the same on any two occasions—outside the office. Nor did she understand herself. She had been angry with him for days, angrier this evening than she had been about anything at all for years, yet it made no difference to the physical attraction she felt for him. Cognitive dissonance, they called it, when brain and ears conveyed one set of facts but eyes and instinct conveyed another, quite different.

'Maxine? Say something. Can we try communicating instead of clashing, for a change?'

'Yes, I—I'd like nothing better, actually.' She sat facing him. Maybe, if she was patient, she could sort out all the contradictory information she had about him.

'I'm not here to fight with you, or to fire you,' he began, his voice matter-of-fact now. 'Nor did I take a dislike to you when we met. Indeed I liked what I saw, what I heard. I hoped things would turn out well, that we'd find we could work together. And, in my opinion, we do make a good team.'

A good team? Had he meant that? He seemed to be serious. 'Then why are you always peering at me through that wretched partition?'

'I'm not always doing that. In any case, you're good to look at, doncha know?' he added, grinning.

She ignored his compliment. 'But I—I thought you thought me incompetent.'

'Why?' He was shocked, genuinely. 'What gave you that idea?'

'The phone calls I've cut off and . . .' What? What else had she done wrong, come to think of it? Perhaps Kurt was right, perhaps she was getting paranoid. She looked at him, relaxing somewhat.

As if sensing the change in her he went on. 'So what? You just needed time to get used to the new phones, that's all. I can't fault your work, Maxine. You're fast and efficient, not once have you had to re-type a letter, not once have you failed to pass on messages, to cope in my absence, to answer my questions on any number of matters. Apart from all that, you're adaptable, you coped beautifully in the chaos of the first week, and you've settled into a routine which is far more demanding than your old one. You hadn't been using half your potential, half your initiative with John Dunn. You were wasted on him. I consider myself damned lucky you've stayed on. Why have you—and what were you doing at Dunn & Dunn in the first place?'

She was smiling now. This was high praise indeed! 'Laziness, in a way. Lack of ambition. I like a quiet life.' He deserved the truth so she gave it to him, explaining how she hadn't wanted the challenge of a high-powered job, how she liked the convenience of being so near, the free time it gave her, how she had not wanted, would not have welcomed, added responsibility.

'But that's precisely what you've had working for me. And longer hours to boot. And I warned you.' Kurt was grinning, openly curious. 'So why did you stay on?'

She was grinning, too. 'Because you were a challenge. Not the job, you. You personally were the challenge.'

He was warming to the conversation, smiling broadly and stretching before flinging his leg over the arm of the chair again, as if he were at home. 'Tell me more.'

Why not? She had nothing to lose; he wasn't here to fire her and maybe, maybe she would withdraw her resignation . . . 'Look, you might be here singing my praises now but two weeks ago it was implicit in your attitude that you thought I wasn't up to working with you. Will you deny it?' Her chin lifted and he smiled, shaking his head.

'Then I think we're getting somewhere, Kurt.' At last she sat back and made herself comfortable. 'You

goaded me into action, but I don't regret it because
I've enjoyed the work. I've enjoyed the work but I
have not enjoyed *you*. If...if we are to carry on
working together, there has to be an end to your
sarcasm. And I want an immediate rise; you're ex-
ploiting me abominably and you know it!'

'Anything else?' There was no uncertainty this time,
he was suppressing laughter all right—and only just.
'Perhaps you'd care to tell me how much more money
you want?'

She did. He shook his head. 'You're still selling
yourself short.'

'I—what do you mean, still?'

She listened carefully, her eyebrows shooting up
from time to time as Kurt Raynor said things about
her that she hadn't even known herself. 'You don't
know who you are, Maxine, you don't even know
what you're worth. Think about what you've just told
me. You said you didn't want added responsibility,
you didn't want a challenge—yet you took on that
responsibility and you took up my challenge. And
you've enjoyed yourself. At least, you've enjoyed the
work, you said so in as many words. Now that makes
me think you were discontented before, whether you
realised it or not. I can see a change in you in just
two weeks. You're alive now; you must have been half
asleep before. What did you have in your life? I mean,
what incentives? What did you have to look forward
to when you got out of bed every morning, what
achievements, what satisfaction? Think about it. And
take that indignant look off your face—this is not an
attack, so *don't* regard it as such, please. I'm not
talking to you as an employer, I'm talking to you as
a friend; I hope you'll accept that.'

'OK.' The word came quietly, very quietly. Had Maxine been able to see her own face, she would have seen surprise, confusion, astonishment flitting across her features. 'You've—certainly given me plenty to think about.' And why was he taking this trouble? Why was he so interested in her, in what went on in her life?

'We'll leave it at that for the time being.' Quietly, seriously, he added, 'Except for one thing. Before I get down to business there is one question you can answer now. For my benefit. If you feel inclined to.'

She nodded. Somewhere inside her was a feeling of gratitude towards him. Quite why, she didn't know. 'Go on.'

'Have you been hurt at some point?'

'What kind of hurt?' Heavens, he was shrewd! She knew full well what he meant, she was just stalling, taken aback by his perception.

'In the love stakes, Maxine. In the love stakes.'

She looked down at the carpet. 'No. No, I haven't.'

'You're lying.' It came very quietly and her head snapped up, but Kurt held up a hand before she could say anything. 'Wait, I'll rephrase that. If you're not lying, you certainly are mistaken. What happened?'

She stared at him, wondering how she had been lulled into this conversation. 'I—was engaged, this time last year. He wasn't local, it was a man I'd known a very short time. I met him through a friend and—we thought we fell in love.'

'And?'

'And we were wrong. It was just one of those things, nice while it lasted but without substance, without foundation.'

'Who broke off the engagement?'

Almost inaudibly she said, 'He did.'

'And it did hurt. It did hurt at the time, didn't it?'

She sighed. 'All right, yes, it did. But not for long. It could so easily have happened the other way around, it was just that he was a step ahead of me, that's all. I was over it in no time, I realised quickly it had all been a mistake.'

'You're not looking at me, Maxine. What are you trying to hide?'

She looked at him. 'Nothing.'

Kurt inclined his head. 'Perhaps. I suspect there's more to this, but maybe you can't see that yet. I suggest you look inside yourself. Ask your heart, Maxine, and let it tell you just how much this engagement business has affected you. Try to see the real extent of it.'

'What? I don't know what you mean.'

'You will, if you ask your heart for the answer.'

'The answer to what? What, exactly?'

'The question is, what did you learn, or fail to learn, from this broken engagement, this mistake as you call it? Oh, I know you'll have thought about it, but on this particular matter that probably didn't get you anywhere. On a matter of this nature you really have to go beyond the obvious, beyond mere thinking, in fact you have to leave your reasoning mind out of it.'

She didn't really understand any of this; he had lost her now. It was as if he was gently trying to make her see something, something he already knew but wouldn't say. 'How can I go beyond the obvious, how can I leave my reasoning out of it?'

'I've just told you, there's one sure way to get at the truth. Look inside yourself, get an answer from the heart.'

'But—at the risk of sounding stupid—how does one look inside oneself? How does one get an answer from the heart? I mean, I don't know how to go about it...'

'It's simplicity itself,' he said. 'You sit quietly, alone, somewhere you won't be distracted, you close your eyes and you still your thoughts, as in meditation. You take the time to let your concentration move inwards, downwards, until you are centred in the heart rather than in the head. You become aware of your heartbeat, and beyond that only of silence. In this way, you'll get in touch with the real you, your higher self if you like, that part of you which knows far more than your brain knows. It'll help if you actually put your hand on your heart, your right hand, and use a visualisation technique. Just imagine that a small, beautiful golden ball is spinning over the top of your head, imagine it sinking down inside you, down and down until it's spinning in your heart, under the palm of your hand. Acknowledge the stillness there and enjoy it for a while. Then ask your questions. The answers will come in the form of thoughts but they won't be coming from your conscious mind. The thoughts will think themselves, your own reasoning won't come into it. And when that happens, you'll know you're in touch with the truth.'

Maxine looked at him hard and long, unsure whether he was serious. He was—he wasn't smiling; on the contrary, he was going on to encourage her further. 'It works, Maxine, you'll see. It's something I was taught to do some years ago and I do it often, especially when I have a problem.'

'Maybe I'll try it some time,' she said, 'although I haven't actually got a problem.' She shrugged, glancing at the clock. 'Kurt, it's almost eight, I have to get ready——'

'I know, I'll get to matters of business now: I need your assistance over the next two weeks, assuming you're prepared to stay on. Are you?'

'Yes, of course.' Of course? It was odd the way she'd added that, but it was how she felt; leaving Dunn & Dunn was suddenly the furthest thought from her mind. 'What kind of assistance?'

'I'm going on the road for a couple of weeks, seeing customers, interviewing new sales reps in certain areas. It's mainly Grove Langley business, but naturally I'll be taking orders for our furniture where I can. I was going to take Linda with me, as I normally do, but——'

'Linda Storton, your secretary at Grove Langley?'

He nodded. 'She's very good at her job, as you are. She's set everything up for me, all the appointments, interviews, hotel bookings. Unfortunately she came in with a stinking cold today. By this afternoon we both realised it was more serious. She's got flu, poor dear—she looked dreadful by mid-afternoon and I sent her home. So,' he shrugged, 'I'm in a fix. Will you do it, Maxine? Will you come with me?'

'Of course.' There it was again. Two weeks—it would mean being away for her birthday, but so what? 'Of course I will, I'll look forward to it.'

He grinned at that. 'Mm. Let's see how you feel after the first couple of days. It can be pretty gruelling—we'll be covering a lot of miles.'

'What will Jim do for a secretary?'

'I talked to him tonight, and he'll get one of the typists to help him. Denise Audrey seems a likely choice.'

'Yes, Denise will cope; she would have been my suggestion.'

'There's one more thing. I want to leave on Sunday. I intend to start in Scotland, in Aberdeen, and work my way down the country. Can you manage that or have you got other plans for the day?'

'I can manage.'

'Meaning you'll cancel your plans?'

'Meaning I'm as free as a bird.'

He seemed to consider that, his eyes narrowing a little. 'Are you? What about William Harrison?'

'What about him? This is business; what possible difference could it make to William?'

Kurt didn't answer that, he just looked at her for several seconds, still thoughtful, before getting to his feet. His back was half turned from her when next he spoke, shrugging into his jacket before putting on his overcoat. 'Then I'll leave you to get ready for him. I'll collect you at eight o'clock on Sunday morning— or is that asking too much?'

Maxine laughed. 'Since when did that bother you?'

Suddenly he turned, his eyes locking on to hers across the space of a few feet. 'Maxine——' He changed his mind. Whatever he'd been about to say, he had changed his mind. It was, she thought, something he rarely did to her knowledge. She had never seen him looking uncertain, almost vulnerable, before. She almost encouraged him to go on. Almost. But he got in first anyway, his voice crisp now. 'Eight o'clock it is, then. I'll see you...'

He left, with Maxine on his heels as he headed for the front door. His departure seemed abrupt. No, it felt abrupt. She felt as if much was being left unsaid, too much... and yet a great deal had been said, re-solved. Yes, resolved. She felt good, far happier than she had felt a couple of hours ago. She felt as if she could settle down, finally, that from now on it would be much easier to cope with Kurt. Oh, the work wouldn't be any easier but—but the anger had gone. It would not be true to say she understood him any better, but it would be true to say she had stopped hating him. It would even be true to say she liked him.

Well, more or less...

Her evening with William ought to have been a good one, but before it was over she had decided definitely not to go out with him again. There was still that something missing with William, something not right; for one thing they had nothing meaningful to say to one another. That was why the evening was flat, that was why it lacked sparkle.

Unfortunately, William did not share her feelings. When Maxine made no offer of a cup of coffee when he drove her home, he attempted to invite himself inside. 'I promise not to keep you up too long, Maxine. I'm on duty in the morning, anyway.'

'No, I'd rather you didn't come in,' she told him, firmly but gently. 'I'm very tired, actually.'

He looked at her swiftly, frowning. 'You know, I felt as if you weren't enjoying yourself tonight. In fact, I thought your mind was elsewhere for most of the time.'

It had been. She had been thinking about Kurt Raynor all evening and she was thinking about him still, right now, while William was asking her to go out with him the following night. She declined, explaining that she had to make a very early start on the Sunday, and why.

'You're going to be with Kurt Raynor for two weeks?' He was blatantly disgruntled, which irritated Maxine no end.

'It's business, William.'

'And is that all?'

'Of course that's all! What exactly are you implying?'

'Sorry, I didn't mean—it's just that I'll miss you.' He looked at her curiously, opened his mouth to say something and changed his mind. Nothing else was said, and Maxine assumed that that was the end of her and William. She felt sure he would take the hint and leave things be now, that there was no need actually to tell him not to ring her again.

She finally got into bed at a little after one. It was just as well it was Saturday tomorrow; she was going to take the children out from St Hilda's, but not until mid-morning, so she could still get eight hours' sleep.

Except that thoughts of Kurt kept her awake. She asked herself why she'd spent the entire evening thinking about him. Probably because he had surprised her. He had surprised her before tonight, she reminded herself, but never in such a pleasant way. He was not the insensitive, single-minded man she had thought him to be—not that she knew what he'd been getting at this evening, not exactly. *Had* she been discontented? She supposed so. Which reminded her of another strange thing he'd said—that he could see a change in her in just two weeks. 'You're alive now,' he'd said, 'you must have been half asleep before.' It was strange because Polly had said something similar.

What were other people seeing that she could not? Kurt, Polly—and anyone else? Had David seen it, too? It was all very interesting, really, even if she couldn't say why. What a curious man Kurt was, all things considered. He was far deeper than she would have imagined, far deeper... Which was all very well, she told herself, but she did not want thoughts of him keeping her from sleep.

It seemed she had no choice in the matter; she tossed and turned, unable to escape her thoughts and wondering what was the matter with her. If she had to reach a conclusion on the thoughts Kurt had provoked, she could do so easily: she had what she wanted and she wanted what she had, a satisfying job *and* the quiet life.

What, then, was keeping her awake?

It was a certain discontent, a new one, that was the nearest she could get to naming it. But why was it there? When had it started? It seemed unfair, illogical. In her new-found contentment, what was this new discontent she could not put her finger on?

CHAPTER FIVE

'How was the party on Friday?'

'Fine. Noisy, the usual sort of party.' Maxine glanced sideways at Kurt. They were in his dark blue Rolls-Royce and they had been travelling for just ten minutes. He had arrived on her doorstep precisely at eight o'clock, just as she had finished writing an explanatory note to Polly, predictably punctual. If only he were predictable in other respects, she thought, glancing at him again.

'Is that all you're telling me? Doesn't sound as if you enjoyed it very much.'

'It was fun,' she said, trying to inject some enthusiasm into her voice. She could hardly tell him the truth—that she had spent the entire evening thinking about him.

'And William? How is William?'

'Fine.'

'And fun?'

'William is . . . a very nice man.'

Kurt took his eyes from the road to look at her. 'Is that all, Maxine? If I remember correctly,' he went on before she could answer, 'you told me during our very first conversation that there was no man in your life. I didn't take you for a liar.'

'I didn't lie, I'd only just met William then—and for the record it's already finished, I shan't be going out with him again.'

'You don't say?'

She looked at him quickly, wondering why he showed no surprise. 'What's that supposed to mean?'

'You told me that you and William were friends.'

'Well, we are. I mean we will be—just because I'm not dating him any more, it doesn't mean we're no longer friends.' She turned to look out of the window, forgetting William, brooding instead on the events of yesterday. 'Yesterday was rotten.' She said it without thinking, was surprised when Kurt laughed.

'That was the most unsubtle change of subject I've ever heard!'

'I wasn't changing the subject. Why should I?'

'Because you don't want to tell me your reasons for breaking it off with the good doctor. But that's OK, I think I know the way your mind works.' He had slowed the car to let a herd of cows cross the road and was nodding to the farmer rather than looking at her. It was impossible to read his expression, to begin to understand what he was getting at. 'No answer, Maxine? OK, then, we'll talk about yesterday's weather.'

'I wasn't talking about the weather, Kurt, I was going to tell you what a rotten day *I* had.'

'You were missing me, were you?'

She couldn't help laughing. He had turned to her with the question, his face a picture of innocence, his dark brown eyes were wide, impassive and—in the broad light of day—beautiful. She hadn't noticed they were beautiful before, nor had she noticed quite how unusual the colour of his hair was, like dark gold sand. It was brushed back from his face and it was tamed, unlike her own, thick and straight except where it curled at the bottom.

She shook herself, embarrassed by her own blatant scrutiny of him. Her laughter had faded in those moments, and it was he who was laughing now, aware of the flush on her cheeks, of her discomfiture. When she dragged her eyes away from him he laughed aloud. 'Why are you blushing, Maxine?'

She turned back to face him, her tongue clicking in irritation. 'Because you bring out the worst in me.'

'Not true! Look how you've blossomed under my care.'

'Care? Care! You're little more than a slave-driver! Look, we can drive on. The cows——'

'Hmm?' Kurt made no move, the car remained stationary and he didn't shift his position. His arm was slung carelessly across the steering-wheel, his left hand on the gear lever, his eyes fixed determinedly on her. They seemed almost to be touching her.

'I . . . said we can drive on. The cows have gone.'

'Uh-huh. Tell me, do you always look this good first thing in the morning, all sparkling blue eyes and golden hair—and pink cheeks?' he added deliberately.

'Yes. I mean no. I mean I look as I usually look, it isn't for me to say whether it's good or not.'

'Then take my word for it,' he said, 'you look good. Now then, what about this rotten day of yours?' He put the car in motion and eased it gently along the country lanes.

Maxine had to concentrate her thoughts; they were scattering every which way. She was thinking that he looked good, too. He always had but—there was something added today. The morning light, perhaps? Beyond that thought was a question, one that had been in need of an answer from the moment she had got into the car with him, from the moment she had felt the effect of this proximity to him: had she made a mistake in agreeing to go on the road with him? She had voluntarily placed herself in his company for far more than the eight hours of a normal working day. They would, she presumed, be dining together, breakfasting together...

'Maxine? Speak to me, woman!'

'What? Oh, yes.' Yesterday seemed unimportant all of a sudden; it seemed like months ago. 'It was just that I took the children out from St Hilda's and their wretched minibus broke down on me. I took them into the countryside to see what's left of the snow and——'

'Did you say St Hilda's? The orphanage?'

'Yes. You know of it? Obviously you know of it!' She paused, waiting for a comment, but none was forthcoming. 'Anyway, the bus broke down in the middle of nowhere and I had to walk for miles before I could phone for help. Mind you, it wasn't the first time it's broken down on me. It's getting past it, St Hilda's have certainly had their money's worth from it—but they can't afford a new one. Not at the moment, so they tell me. It's a case of make do and mend. Where was I? Oh, yes, in the middle of nowhere! Well, I didn't know what to do, whether to take the children with me or leave them in the bus. In the end——'

'Why do you do that?' Kurt interrupted her, his voice almost sharp. 'You do it voluntarily? You take the children out in your spare time?'

'Well, yes. I don't see why you're——' Why you're so surprised, she would have said, had he given her the chance.

'But why?' he insisted.

'Why not? I happen to like children, very much. Quite apart from that, they're always glad of some help—they seem to be constantly short-staffed.' It was true. St Hilda's was one of several children's homes run by a charity whose funds were by no means limitless.

'You mean it gives you something to do?'

Maxine frowned. 'No, I don't mean that. I mean what I say, I like children, it's as simple as that.'

'You must love children.'

'All right, I love children.' Why was he reacting like this? 'Is that so unusual in a person? You're reacting as if I'd said something abnormal rather than normal, perfectly normal. Yes, I do love children, I love the way they see things with such simplicity, the way their perceptions are so different from adults', uncluttered, fresh. I love their eager young minds, their thirst for knowledge. I think that answers your question.'

'Yes, it does,' he said quietly. 'More than.'

Which was, Maxine realised, her cue to stop going on. She also realised that he obviously didn't care at all for children, that he really couldn't understand why she spent time at the orphanage. Again she turned to look out of the window, knowing a sense of disappointment she couldn't begin to explain.

They were on open roads now, the Rolls coming into its own as Kurt accelerated and let the engine do its work. The sound of other traffic was so dim that one had to listen for it. Maxine tried to relax and enjoy the quietness, the comfort and luxury of the big car.

When he told her they were stopping for lunch she was surprised; time had flown. She watched him, her eyes drawn involuntarily as he walked around the car to open the door for her. Little things. She had wondered whether he would do this, and he did. It pleased her. It worried her, too, when he held the door open and let his eyes travel the length of her, lingering on her long legs as she swung them out of the car. Worse, he placed himself in such a position that she was standing very close to him when she straightened up, closer than was necessary. Too close for comfort.

Without warning her heart started beating stupidly, crazily fast, and it was not helped by the ripple of annoyance that ran through her. Was he doing this on purpose? Was he aware of the physical attraction he held for her? Determinedly she averted her eyes, side-stepping so he could close the door behind her.

Soft, quiet laughter reached her, then his arm was on hers and he was tucking it under his, laughing down at her as they began to cross the car park. He pre-empted her protest, flashing that smile which changed his features and lit up his eyes. 'It's icy, you'd better hold on to me. Never let it be said, Miss Smith, that the age of chivalry has gone.'

They kept strictly to business during lunch. Or rather, Kurt talked business so Maxine followed his lead, asking him questions about the kitchen fitments Grove Langley manufactured. She had been wrong in thinking them all cheap and nasty; they ranged from cheap to middle of the market, self-assembly or professionally fitted, and Kurt was planning a new line of luxury custom-made kitchens with all the trim-mings one could wish for. 'This is what I'm going to talk to customers about—the new range. I want to get a feel for the likely demands in different areas.'

'Is that why you're making this trip personally? I mean, you have salesmen to——'

'Yes, yes, but customers like to see me from time to time. I'm also looking for business for Dunn & Dunn, remember; some of the department stores we'll be visiting also stock our furniture and that's where you'll be able to help.'

They got to Aberdeen late on the Sunday evening, by which time Maxine was shattered from the drive, a very long drive through all kinds of weather, mostly *un*kind. In Scotland it was bitterly cold; they had approached Aberdeen through thick snow lying crisply in the countryside and as slush in the towns. But she wasn't too tired to worry, to think about her situation when she and Kurt were shown to the suite of rooms Linda Storton had reserved for them. For Kurt and for Linda herself, actually. Would his secretary at Grove Langley have had qualms about sharing a suite with her boss? Maybe she had done so before, maybe she had done so several times... That provoked a thought, a question: how long had Linda worked for Kurt and what was their relationship, exactly?

Maxine stepped out of her shoes and looked around at her temporary home, acknowledging how little she knew about Kurt. He might work hard and long, but there was room for women in his life. The memory of the tall blonde she had seen him with in the Copper Kettle was still very fresh in her mind. Who was she? What did she mean to him? And were there any other women in his life?

She glanced at him as he flung his jacket over the back of a chair, telling herself not to worry so much. In any case, his attitude towards her had changed; it was as if, from lunchtime onwards, he had once again ceased to notice that she was a woman. He was all business, strictly business, even when he invited her to have a nightcap with him in their sitting-room.

'How about ringing room service, having a nightcap before we turn in?' He glanced at his watch, frowning. 'The drive took longer than I anticipated, thanks to the weather. You won't get a full night's sleep tonight, Maxine; we'll be up early in the morning and you'd best prepare yourself for some hard work.'

He wasn't even looking at her, and she watched him as he loosened his tie, thinking she might just as well be invisible for all the notice he was taking of her. He didn't actually want her company any longer, he was just being polite. Well, that was fine by her. She was desperate for some sleep in any case.

'I'll pass on the drink, thank you.' She glanced in the direction of her room, knowing she simply must unpack her clothes and dreading the effort it would take. 'I'll—see you in the morning, Kurt.'

They visited shops and stores in Aberdeen, Dundee, Perth, Stirling, Glasgow and Edinburgh over the next few days, changing hotels once, and Maxine's boss did not waste one minute of their time. Even during the obligatory luncheons with certain customers she was on duty, having to look good and make appropriate conversation. During a typical day she was handing out brochures and the promotional material Kurt had taken with him, she was writing down orders, making notes of complaints or criticisms, getting telephone numbers for him when they were back in the hotel, taking messages, organising coffee and snacks and, in the evening, greeting and seating the men who had been lined up for interviews—prospective sales representatives. All this, quite apart from the miles they covered between calls, all the packing and unpacking when they changed hotels again.

There was no time for conversations on a personal level, even if either of them had felt so inclined. At the end of the day—the end of the night, more like—Kurt did invite her to have a drink with him, either in the downstairs bars or in their sitting-room, but by that time Maxine was too tired for anything except bed. She always declined politely, with a smile. 'You go ahead, Kurt. I want to ring Polly then take a bath and get my beauty sleep.'

It was, as he had warned her, hard work. But she was enjoying herself enormously in spite of the intensity of their itinerary. Watching Kurt Raynor in action was an entertainment in itself; he knew how to handle people, and he never seemed to lack energy or enthusiasm. And he was well-liked, respected; buyers greeted him as though he were an old friend and Maxine was, she realised, beginning to like him very much herself—more than she wanted to and possibly more than was good for her, because there were a few times when his indifference to her at a personal level came close to hurting her. It was on the occasions when they touched, just the inevitable and meaningless kind of contact, be it the brush of a hand or an arm. She would almost jump at the contact, while Kurt never even noticed. He might not be aware of her as a woman, but she was certainly aware of him as a man.

At the crack of dawn on the Saturday morning, a very wet dawn, she woke from a dream which had featured him. The details of it were immediately lost to her but it had been disturbing, she remembered that much. She remembered also that they had a particularly early start that day and flung herself out of bed feeling disorientated and vaguely unhappy.

An hour later she and Kurt were on the road again, this time heading in the direction of Wolverhampton. Maxine was consulting their itinerary. 'I see you're interviewing people this morning, Kurt, but—there's nothing here for this afternoon.'

'What?' He was concentrating on his driving. It was pelting with rain, coming down in sheets, and the windscreen wipers were having trouble coping with it.

'I said, am I right in thinking we've got a free afternoon?'

'You are.' There was a smile in his voice but he didn't turn to look at her. 'And tomorrow. There's not much we can do on a Sunday.'

'We could go home for the weekend, we're in easy driving distance. If we left after lunch we——'

'That is *not* part of my plan. We're driving to Wales straight after lunch and *that's* where we're spending our free time.'

She blinked in surprise, taken aback by his attitude. 'OK. I was only thinking——'

'You don't want to spend the weekend with me, is that it?'

'No! I didn't say that.'

'Look at Monday morning,' he said stiffly, 'if you haven't looked already.'

She hadn't. She looked through the remaining pages of the itinerary Linda Storton had prepared and discovered that on Monday they would be working in north Wales. After that they were making their way down to Cardiff and Swansea, then they'd cross the Severn Bridge and head for Bristol. After that . . . she didn't get any further. Kurt was cursing under his breath, and a moment later he pulled off the road and parked in a lay-by. The rain was coming in torrents now, and as soon as he cut the engine Maxine heard the first rumble of thunder.

'Gosh! I—I don't think I've ever seen it raining this hard.' She was looking out of the side window, astonished because she couldn't actually see anything but the rain racing down it. On the roof of the car was a rapid drumming noise, and even as she watched and listened the heavens opened and lightning cracked in a jagged line across the sky. She jumped nervously, not at all thrilled at the idea of being in a car while this was going on. 'Are we—safe in here?'

'Perfectly. Relax. You're safe in the car and you're safe with me, OK?'

The tone of his voice brought her head around. One look at his face and her heart sank. What had she done? Everything had gone beautifully so far—they had performed their roles as employer and employee without a hitch, without a cross word, without sarcasm, aggression, defensiveness, anything. Now, however, they were two personalities again, two individuals. Man and woman. There was tension in the air and it was not emanating solely from Maxine.

Kurt released their safety belts, then he pressed a button that eased his seat back and suggested she did the same. 'Might as well stretch out a bit—I've no intention of driving on in this. We might be here for quite a while.'

Maxine said nothing. She felt ridiculously upset, not knowing what she had done wrong. Surely it hadn't been her suggestion that they went home for the weekend? Inside the car all was silent as the minutes ticked by. It was an awkward silence and it was she who broke it, she who was unable to stand it. 'Kurt, what have I done? What have I said?'

It was seconds before he answered and when he did so he took her by surprise. 'What have you said? Well now, let's see—it sounded to me as if you can't wait to get out of my company, it sounded to me as if you're homesick or something. It sounded—— '

'That's ridiculous! That is wholly in your imagination. I was merely——'

'Ridiculous, is it? In my imagination?' His voice, deep in any case, seemed even deeper now, as if he was not fully in control of it. In other words he was angry, she could see it in his eyes, in the set of his mouth, in the clenched fingers he had curled around the steering-wheel. 'As far as work is concerned, I cannot fault you, *Miss Smith*. You've been indispensable, superb, you've managed to anticipate my needs all along the line, but that's *all* you've been prepared to do—your duty! At the end of the day you couldn't wait to get away from me. Or was it in my imagination that you refused each and every time I asked you to have a drink with me? Did I imagine that every time I touched you even in the smallest way you recoiled? Have I been hallucinating all that, and the anxious looks I've seen in your eyes? Let me tell you, this week has been unprecedented in my life. I have never been treated to such a peculiar mixture of willingness and unwillingness, of friendliness and stand-offishness all at the same time. Frankly, I don't know how you do it. Frankly, I don't know where the hell I am with you and, *frankly*, I'm sick of it!'

Maxine could do no more than stare at him. Had he not been so furious she might have laughed. She might have laughed at the misunderstandings which had, evidently, been going on between them all week. So he had noticed her reaction whenever they touched—but he didn't realise it was involuntary, that she hadn't deliberately recoiled from him, as he seemed to think. Nor had she wilfully refused to have drinks with him. She hadn't been avoiding him, she had thought he was just being polite, doing *his* duty by her in asking her to relax with him.

She plunged into an explanation as best she could without letting him know all that was going on from her point of view. She could hardly tell him that this very morning she had woken from a vivid dream about him and that she had, albeit briefly, had the crazy notion that she might be falling in love with him. Naturally she had dismissed the idea at once. Falling in love again was the last thing she wanted right now, and most especially with such an unknown quantity of a man.

So she told him what she could; in an effort to maintain at least a surface peace she explained that he had misunderstood her totally. 'And so I thought,' she said at length, 'that you were merely being polite.'

He looked cynical but, finally, he seemed to believe her. 'All right. Maybe I let it blow up out of proportion.'

Was that an apology? She treated it as such. 'That's all right. It's called lack of communication.'

'Don't I know it!' Again he exploded, turning to face her fully. 'And it seems to have dogged us both from day one, does it not? Well, it's time we stopped using words, since they're obviously so inadequate.'

That was all the warning she had. Her lips parted with a gasp, her blue eyes widening as Kurt gathered her roughly in his arms and brought his mouth down on hers. For several seconds, in shock, she struggled against him. But it was pointless, he held her so tightly, his mouth almost punishing as he plundered hers, his tongue probing audaciously, relentlessly, exploring the moist warmth of her mouth.

Then suddenly everything changed for Maxine. There was a different kind of shock, the shock of her body coming instantly, vibrantly alive; there was the tingling shock of excitement rushing to every limb; there was the thud of her heart against his chest— being met with the rapid thud of his as he held her impossibly close. How long it took for common sense to return, she didn't know. Seconds, minutes—the kiss seemed to go on and on and on. Then his mouth moved from her lips to her throat, his free hand caught hold of her hair, quite brutally, making it impossible for her to move her head. 'Kurt, please...' But he ignored the plea, his mouth returning to hers with a force that would not be denied.

Maxine's head was swimming. Everything seemed unreal—the rush and drumming of the rain, the crash of thunder, the flash of lightning—everything except her arousal. Everything except Kurt. But it was real, all of it, she was in a car in the middle of nowhere, being kissed passionately, devastatingly, by a man she was trying to think of as nothing other than her boss. Panic brought her to her senses, giving her the strength to wrench away from him. 'Kurt, let go of me! I don't want——'

'What?' he demanded. His face was only inches from hers, and his fingers slid back into her hair and tightened cruelly, forcing her head to tilt until she could not avoid looking at him. 'What don't you want? This? Me? Don't you think you've made that perfectly clear already? Have you any idea how much I *have* wanted this? How much I've wanted to kiss you, to take you in my arms and hold you?'

'You're hurting me...' It was all she could say, all she could think of. His words had and had not penetrated. Everything was coming at her too fast, his change of mood, his onslaught, his questions. 'Kurt, *please*!'

He let go of her, shoving himself back to sit half facing her, half leaning against the door. One hand went up to push back the thick, sand-coloured hair where it had fallen over his brow, and in the seconds while this was happening Maxine struggled for composure, for air—for inspiration. The silence was screaming at her now and she didn't know how they would break it, how things could possibly get back to normal.

'I'm not going to apologise.' Kurt's voice was like gravel when finally he spoke. 'We've come close to this before, Maxine, and when that happened you made it abundantly clear you wanted neither my kiss nor my touch. *But——*' suddenly his hand snaked out to catch hold of her chin '—it was a lie! Oh, the alarm was real enough—all that I've read in your eyes this week, and before, all that was real enough. But we've just got at the truth in a way that was far more re-vealing than words could ever be—you don't want to want me, yet you're just as attracted to me as I am to you. Now, are you going to deny it? Are we going to prolong the misunderstandings? Or worse, try de-liberately to deceive?'

'No.' It came from her as a whisper, but he caught it.

'No? Do you think you could bring yourself to en-large on that?'

She did, but she couldn't look at him. As if she were giving answers in an oral examination, she spoke flatly, matter-of-factly. 'No, I'm not going to deny it. Yes, I am attracted to you. And yes, you're right in saying that I don't want to be.'

'And why is that?' His voice was surprisingly soft now. She still didn't turn to look at him, but she could have sworn he was smiling.

'Do I really have to put into words that which should be obvious to you? You're my boss, my em-ployer, and I don't want to get involved with you.'

'Why not?'

Maxine stared at him, unable to believe his persis-tence, unable to believe he needed any further explanation. Exasperated, she threw up her hands. 'I just *don't*.'

'That isn't good enough. I want to know why. Does being your employer make me a second-class citizen or something?'

'No, of course not——'

'Of course not,' he parroted. 'Then what's the real reason for your reluctance?'

'All right. It's because I am wary, very wary, when it comes to getting involved with a man—any man.'

'Ah! I think we're finally getting somewhere. The night I came to your house to see if you would make this trip with me, I asked you what you'd learned from your experience with what's-his-name, your broken engagement. Can you answer that now?'

'For heaven's sake, I just *did*! This isn't news to me, Kurt. I could have answered you then but you wouldn't let me.'

'No, because, as I told you, there's more to it than that, more to it than the obvious. I wanted you to search your heart for the answers. Didn't you do that?'

'I didn't have to,' she snapped. 'I understand myself much better than you seem to think. I made a mistake twelve months ago and the effect has been to make me cautious. I learned my lesson very well.'

'No, that's just where you're wrong.' Kurt spoke quietly, his look meaningful as he switched on the engine and put the car into drive. 'That's just where you're quite, quite wrong, Maxine.'

CHAPTER SIX

'POLLY? It's me. How're you getting on?'

Polly's laughter came trilling down the telephone. 'I'm all right. More to the point, how are *you* getting on?'

Maxine put her feet up on the bed, relieved and grateful for the few hours of freedom she had before dinner. She and Kurt had left Wolverhampton straight after lunch and were now at an old inn in Wales, in the heart of Snowdonia, comfortably accommodated in adjoining bedrooms.

'Max? I said how are you getting on with that gorgeous boss of yours? Is he still running you off your feet?'

'You could say that, Polly, you could say that.' Maxine was doodling on the little pad by the side of the telephone, wishing Polly were in the room with her. There was so much she wanted to say about Kurt but talking over the phone was too limiting. Besides, she'd had to make this call via the switchboard downstairs so she couldn't be absolutely sure it was private—someone might be listening in. 'Put it this way, I've earned my pay this week. This afternoon we drove to north Wales, that's where I'm calling from, and we've got tomorrow free.'

'So what does he intend to do with the day?'

'I have no idea.' Maxine knew only that she and Kurt would be alone tonight, which would make a change. He had asked her to be ready to go downstairs at eight o'clock.

'By the way,' Polly went on, 'William Harrison phoned. He wanted me to give him a number where he could reach you.'

'William? Whatever for?'

'Don't know. Maybe he's missing you. Anyhow, I said I'd have to check with you first, I said you might be too busy.'

'Good. If he rings again, tell him I'll be home on Saturday and he can talk to me then—if he must.'

When she finished her call to Polly, Maxine undressed and got into bed for a nap. She took the precaution of setting her travelling alarm clock for seven and sank back against the pillows, convinced she would fall asleep without any trouble.

She did not fall asleep without trouble, the trouble being that her mind seemed determined to review her relationship with Kurt whether she liked it or not.

Of course he had known. Looking back, it was obvious he'd known all along that she was attracted to him. She had to admit that he understood her quite well. As for him, well, she really knew very little about him except that he was constantly surprising her, that she was seeing new sides to his character daily. Lord, he had been so persistent today, when she had been with him in the car, in the storm, trapped by his incessant questioning. She had to say one thing for him: Kurt Raynor was a very determined man. But what did he want of her, actually...?

When the alarm rang at seven, that question was still in her mind, still unanswered. She got out of bed, took a quick shower and, while doing her make-up, thought about what she would wear. She didn't have many clothes with her—not clothes that were suitable for an evening here; the things she had worn on previous evenings had been brought in the knowledge that she would be staying in places far more swish and she didn't want to be overdressed. Nor did she want to dress like a secretary.

After a long, thoughtful stare at the contents of the wardrobe, she found a compromise. There was a plain white sweater she had not yet worn; that combined with a straight black skirt would do nicely if she softened the look with her broad, red leather belt. After the addition of some gold chains at her neck, with matching earrings, she went through the usual fight with her unruly curls and left her hair loose. It would do its own thing anyway.

Kurt's reaction when he came for her was one of open admiration. 'Very nice, Maxine. You should wear your hair loose always. You look very stern when it's scraped back in a knot.'

She tried not to laugh. 'I can look very stern when it's down, so you'd better be on your best behaviour tonight.'

'Why, Maxine! Aren't I always?' He took her hand as they made their way down to the bar, and she let him, but she didn't compliment him on his appearance, despite his looking extremely attractive. He, too, had compromised with his clothes, he wore a navy suit with a very fine, pale blue polo-neck sweater.

Over pre-dinner drinks she told him the news Polly had passed on. 'The police went to see her yesterday. They've caught our burglars.'

'Really? I'm very glad to hear it.'

'So am I. And guess what?' Maxine shook her head, still finding it difficult to credit what she had been told. 'There were two of them—and they were aged fifteen and seventeen.'

Kurt smiled at her. 'If you're expecting me to be shocked, I'm not.'

'But isn't it awful? So young?'

'Are they local lads?'

'No. It seems they were picked up in London yesterday, driving a stolen car, only just stolen—its owner had reported it missing only two hours earlier. The police were really on the ball. They hauled the boys in and took their fingerprints, and they matched with the perfect prints the police got in our living-room. Just for good measure, the seventeen-year-old didn't even have a driving licence.'

'So that's that.' Kurt signalled the waiter for more drinks. There were only a few people in the bar, seven including themselves. Within half an hour several more appeared, people who were not residents, who had come for dinner. From where, and how far they had driven was anyone's guess. As far as Maxine was concerned there was no civilisation around for miles.

'How's Polly getting on?' Kurt wanted to know. 'Is she missing you?'

'Of course not, she has David!'

'Ah, yes. Have those two named the big day yet?'

'They'll probably get married during the summer of next year.'

'Next year? Why so far off? I thought long engagements were out these days.'

'They are for the most part, but my sister is a very practical person and it's a question of money. She and David are saving for their own home. Meantime— well, there's no mortgage on our house and David's rent is very cheap, so they might as well save all they can.'

Over dinner Maxine regretted her two earlier drinks. Her second glass of wine, combining with gin and tonic, was making itself felt. 'That's it, Kurt.' She put her hand over her glass, giggling. 'It's up to you now.

I'm already talking too much and I've started giggling.'

'Is that a bad sign?' He looked at her so gravely he set her off again.

'Definitely! See?'

'I see. And I like what I see.' His hand reached for hers across the small table, a circular one in the corner of the room, and the contact was shocking to her. Suddenly the restaurant was taking on an intimacy she hadn't noticed earlier, the candles on the tables, the flowers, the soft, concealed lighting...

'I've never seen you this relaxed,' Kurt went on, his fingers curling around hers. 'I approve.'

'That's—nice.' She almost flinched at her trite reply. If one of them didn't change the subject, she wouldn't be relaxed for much longer. 'Tell me about yourself,' she said brightly, easing her hand with apparent casualness from his. 'Tell me all about yourself. Do you realise how little I know about you?'

'You know a lot about me.'

'Oh, Kurt, you know what I mean.'

He also knew what she was doing; his eyes were laughing at her. 'So you want to talk about me? Anything rather than talk about you, eh? Very well. Supposing you ask questions and I answer them.'

'Right. Where were you born?'

'In Scotland, in Edinburgh.'

'But how come—haven't you got family there? Why didn't you visit——'

'I have no family.'

'Your parents are both dead?'

'My mother is. I don't know about my father. I never knew him, Maxine, he never married my mother. I know very little at all about him.'

The news took her by surprise but she wasn't going to ask how he felt about his missing father—she could guess that much.

'So you have no one? Not even an aunt or a cousin or——'

'No one at all.' The answer came quietly.

'I'm—sorry, Kurt, I didn't mean to pry.'

To her relief he smiled. 'You weren't, you were invited to ask and there's no need to stop.'

'OK, so you were brought up in Scotland. And then what?'

'When I left school, at sixteen, I took a very ordinary job in a store.' His first job had in fact been at one of the stores they had visited. He volunteered that after hesitating, as if he had wondered whether or not to tell her.

'Let me guess!' Maxine was intrigued. 'You weren't by any chance selling kitchen furniture, were you?'

She regretted her flippant tone immediately. Kurt glanced away briefly. 'Yes, I was. I was a general dogsbody. After three months of it I left and went to work in a factory—a factory that made the furniture the store was then selling. I'd had only a basic education so I continued to educate myself at night and I worked hard at my job during the day.'

Maxine fell quiet, her expression intense. Why had she assumed he'd had a different background? Because of his fine intelligence? She had assumed him well educated, which he was—but only thanks to his own efforts. And there was his voice, too, accentless, deep, precise, cultured. 'I have to say I'm astonished. I never thought—well, would it be rude to say you had a poor upbringing?' She was waiting for the story of his subsequent success but he chose to skip most of the details.

'No, it would be accurate. When I was twenty-one I moved south, and shortly after that I won some money—on the football pools, would you believe? It was quite a large sum, or so it seemed to me at the time.'

'And you used it to set up a business?'

'Not quite, I bought into a business. It didn't become wholly mine for some time.'

That had to be Grove Langley. Maxine remembered Jim Ferguson telling her how Kurt had contacted him after years of not seeing him, when Kurt was twenty-five, when the business was established and he had offered Jim a job.

'Hey, where have you gone?' Kurt was teasing her, his hand reaching over to cup her chin.

'I'm here,' she said softly, her eyes meeting his. 'And I was just thinking, you're full of surprises and you're really rather nice, after all.'

'We-ell! If I'd known that's what my story would do to you, I would have told you days ago...' He smiled, leaning back in his chair as if he could gauge her better from a little distance. His gaze took in everything, her expression, the look in her eyes, and gradually the smile faded from his face. 'Your compliment pleases me very much, Maxine.'

It was her turn to smile, a self-mocking smile. 'And heaven knows you've waited long enough for a compliment from me.'

'True, true.' It drew a laugh from him. He laughed again when he saw her yawning. 'What would you like to do tomorrow? Have a lie-in, I suppose?'

'Mmm. What I'd really like to do is sleep until nature wakes me.'

'And so you shall. I'll be around, come and find me when you're ready.'

When she yawned again, he suggested they call it a day. 'I was about to suggest we went to bed,' he told her, 'but I thought I'd better choose my words more carefully.' His dark eyes were glittering with laughter; he was waiting for a retort she didn't make. 'What? No shock horror, Maxine? In that case, shall we go to bed, then?'

'If you mean,' she said, refusing to rise to the bait, 'that you think it's time we retired, then I'm in full agreement.'

'And I,' he said, getting up and holding her chair for her, 'shall consider myself put firmly in my place.'

She took the hand he held out to her, tucking her small clutch bag under her other arm. 'Oh, really? You never have in the past.'

'You know, Miss Smith, you can be exceedingly facetious at times.'

'When you work with gold,' she pointed out, smiling up at him as they climbed the stairs, 'some of it's bound to rub off.'

His appreciative laughter set her off giggling again. She turned to him when they reached the door of her room, eyes bright, her face slightly flushed.

Kurt looked down at her, sobering as his eyes met hers. 'Lord, you're so beautiful...'

'No, I'm not beautiful. I...' What? What did she want to say? I'm nervous, you're about to kiss me and it makes me nervous because I want it so much, so very much...

'Still wary?' It was as if he had read her mind. 'Come here, Maxine.' He caught hold of her as she turned away, his hand light on her shoulder. It was the merest touch but she stiffened as if it had burnt her. 'Kiss me,' he said. 'I want you to kiss me goodnight.'

For seconds she could do no more than look at him, her mind racing frantically. On the one hand she was telling herself to break free, that if she did as he asked she would be going against what she had said earlier in the day. On the other hand she was telling herself that a goodnight kiss hardly amounted to involvement, that there would be no harm at all in a simple kiss. Would there?

She found out when she kissed him, standing on her toes, her arms linked around his neck. It did begin as a simple kiss—until Kurt took control, until he closed his arms around her and pulled her tightly against his body, his mouth becoming hungry on hers. He kissed her with a passion she immediately reciprocated in spite of herself. At that point, while she was still able to think, she quickly pulled away and turned her back on him.

From behind her his voice sounded vaguely amused. 'Is that it, Maxine?'

'That's it. I—really must get some sleep.'

'You didn't sleep this afternoon, then?'

She didn't turn to look at him. 'I—a little.'

'I couldn't sleep at all; thoughts of you kept me awake.'

'I'm sorry to hear that. Goodnight, Kurt.'

'Sorry?' he said. 'Why? If I'm not, why should you be?'

'You know the answer to that.'

'Ah, yes, your reluctance to get involved. Tell me, Maxine, this fear of——'

Angrily she spun around. 'Don't! Don't start on that again. I am as I am, just accept that, stop trying to change me. I am afraid of involvement, and that's that. Because involvement can lead to commitment—and *that* terrifies me!'

'Well done,' he said, smiling as if she had passed some sort of test. He waited, seeming sure she would add something, which she didn't, not until he prompted her. 'I have a question.'

'So what's new?'

'Don't be sarcastic, this is for your benefit, not mine. I'd like to know if your fears are such that you intend to live the rest of your life like a nun.'

Maxine fixed her eyes on the wallpaper behind him. She had no idea how to answer that; she had never actually thought about it.

'Think about it,' he advised, 'and do bear in mind that I haven't asked you for anything, most especially any kind of commitment. Goodnight, Maxine.'

She let herself into her room, swung the door shut quietly and leaned against it. For reasons she couldn't begin to understand, tears were stinging her eyes. Her fingers moved to her lips, pressing against them, while the question Kurt had asked kept repeating itself in her mind.

It was eleven o'clock when she woke the next morning. She couldn't believe it was that late; she showered and dressed and went in search of Kurt.

He wasn't in his room. He wasn't in the inn, and the receptionist told her he'd gone out for a walk some time ago, so she waited by the huge fire in the bar, sipping coffee and wondering what sort of mood he was in this morning.

When he came to her he was smiling. 'Hi! It's a beautiful day. At least, it is now,' he added, his eyes roving appreciatively over her. 'Is there any more coffee in that pot?'

'Lots.' She felt ludicrously pleased by his compliment. 'It's good news about the weather. About

time, too—a few more days and we'll be in March.'
A few more days and it would be her birthday, but
she wasn't going to mention that. 'It's been a long
winter.'

'So, what would you like to do?' Kurt settled
himself in a chair beside her. 'Anything in particular?'

'What I'd really like to do,' she said, remembering
where they were, 'is drive round the mountain. I've
never actually been up Mount Snowdon and——' She
stopped, realising how thoughtless she was being. Kurt
had had more than enough driving to do already and
there was a lot more to come.

'And?'

'And there again, perhaps not. I think we should
sit around and relax.'

He laughed at her. 'Maxine, when are you going to
realise what a lousy liar you are, that your feelings
show in your eyes, that I can read you like a book?'

'I don't know,' she said quietly. 'When am I?'

'So Mount Snowdon it is—provided you're prepared to do the driving.'

'*Me?*' In his car? A Rolls-Royce, for heaven's sake!
'There's no way I could drive your car!'

'Why not?'

'It's too—big.'

'Rubbish. If you can drive a minibus, you can drive
a Rolls. You'll be amazed how easy it is to handle—
it's got power-assisted everything.'

'But—it's too—what I'm trying to say is that I'd
be terrified of crunching it.'

'You won't. Why should you? Besides, what's there
to crunch it on? A few mountain sheep? It won't exactly be like the M1 up there, you know.'

'I realise that, but it could be treacherous, all twisty-
windy.'

'True, true.' He wasn't taking her seriously. 'But don't let that throw you.'

'But—you've never asked me to drive before.'

'Ah, today's different. Today we're not in a hurry to get anywhere.'

She answered that with a dig in the ribs. 'What a nerve. Typical male!'

Kurt was right, the big car was astonishingly easy to handle. Within five minutes, after her initial nervousness wore off, Maxine warmed to her task and decided she could get used to driving a Rolls-Royce. Definitely!

It was a cold day, but it was gorgeous, sunny, such a contrast to yesterday's rain. It was a contrast in many ways—both she and Kurt were completely relaxed, talking about anything and everything, as if they had known each other for years rather than weeks. They stopped in Betws-y-Coed and walked for a while.

'The Welsh air agrees with you,' he said as they strolled. 'You've got that delightful pink glow on your face.'

'Oh!' She glared at him. He knew how to get her goat when he wanted to. 'Just for that, *you* can drive back to the inn.'

'My dear girl, I have every intention of so doing. I doubt you could find your way.'

'Why you—one can go off people, you know!'

'I know, but don't worry, I haven't gone off you. In fact I was thinking of asking you to marry me.'

'Is that a fact? When? This afternoon?'

'Now what are you thinking about, woman? It's Sunday. No one gets married in Wales on a Sunday!'

'Oh, yes, I forgot it was Sunday.' She clicked her fingers before her attention was caught by a little white lamb in the window of a shop selling woollens and Welsh tapestries. 'Oh, look at that! Isn't it *sweet*?'

Kurt looked heavenward, grinning. 'I'm afraid you'll have to live without it, they're closed. It's——'

'Sunday.' She linked her arm through his, shrugging philosophically. 'Oh, well, we can't have everything, we can't get married and we can't buy the lamb.'

'Tough, isn't it?'

'Life's like that.'

Back at the inn they sat by the fire and played draughts. When Kurt beat her three games running, Maxine gave up. 'There's Scrabble, too. Give me a chance to get my own back?'

'Certainly, if you insist on being masochistic.'

She wagged a finger at him. 'Don't speak too soon.'

He hadn't—again he beat her three games running and she gave up once and for all. Well, at least for today. 'Some other time,' she said. 'I shall slaughter you.'

'I'll look forward to it.' He looked at his watch. 'It's six-thirty. How long do you need to get ready for dinner?'

'Are we eating in?'

'Not if you'd rather go out.'

'I'd rather stay in. I've had a lovely, lovely day but my energy's run out.' She got to her feet, stretching languorously. Kurt got up, too, his eyes fixed on her and showing their appreciation.

'Any more of that and you'll have my imagination running riot all over again tonight. You don't make it easy for a man to sleep, you know, most especially when he knows you're in bed in the room right next to his . . .'

Maxine let that go without a comment, without any attempt at a witty retort. It was too serious to be treated lightly. Her own imagination had run riot last night, and she didn't want it to happen again tonight.

Back in her room she took that thought further and on doing so she realised with a sense of shock that things had got out of hand. Oh, nothing had happened between her and Kurt ... and yet in a way a great deal had happened. Not only today but every day, one way or another.

'How are you doing?' When Kurt knocked at her door, Maxine jumped, realising she had been sitting very still, staring into space.

'I'm ... I'll be right with you.' Mentally she shook herself, then she grabbed her bag and put a smile on her face before opening her door.

There were only a few people in the restaurant, it being Sunday, just a scattering of residents, out of season holiday-makers, presumably. Maxine and Kurt were at the same corner table, replete and pleasantly mellow by the time coffee was served.

'Are you tired, Maxine?'

'Not a bit,' she smiled. 'Makes a change, doesn't it? No, I'm just feeling content.'

'That's good to hear. How about a nightcap, then? Brandy? Shall we go to the bar for it?'

'Will the bar still be open? I mean, it is——'

'Sunday.' He laughed as he got to his feet. 'Yes. We're resident, that makes drinking on Sunday permissible.'

'OK.' She had had only one glass of wine. Kurt had drunk most of the bottle and she had abstained deliberately, wanting to keep her wits about her. The physical attraction between her and Kurt was crackling every minute of every day, and for her part even more so today.

Kurt excused himself when they walked out of the restaurant. 'You go ahead, Maxine, I'll see you in a couple of minutes.'

She nodded and headed for the bar, making a bee-line for the table nearest the fire. The place was almost deserted and she glanced around, idly wondering whether the inn's owners managed to make any profit during the winter. Her wondering was cut short as her eyes alighted on the man sitting across the room—in fact her breathing was cut short, and she was so stunned that for long seconds everything about her was motionless.

The man had spotted her and was already on his way over, beaming broadly. 'I don't believe this! Here I am in the middle of nowhere—how are you, Maxine?'

'I—I'm . . .'

'As stunned as I am, by the look of it!' Francis Lyon laughed loudly, a sound both familiar and un-familiar. 'It's amazing, isn't it? Fancy running into one another here, of all the God-forsaken places!'

She didn't fancy it, she did not fancy it one bit, but it was happening. With a blank expression on her face she stared up at the man she had once been engaged to—and what she saw was a stranger.

'So how are you doing?' he wanted to know, clearly delighted by this coincidence. He sat down, without reference to her, and offered to buy her a drink.

Why Maxine was panicking, she didn't stop to think, she just was. 'No! I mean, no, thank you. I'm—not alone, actually. I'm with—my boss is with me.'

'Your boss?'

Someone beat her to a reply. It was the man himself, speaking from directly behind her. 'Kurt Raynor.'

Maxine almost fell off her chair, her head snapped round and she was staring up at Kurt, who was smiling as broadly as Francis was. 'Kurt! I didn't see you——'

'Don't get up,' he was saying to the younger man, ignoring the shock on Maxine's face as he held out his hand. 'The name's Raynor, Kurt Raynor. And you are?'

'Francis Lyon.' Francis did get up, just long enough to shake hands with Kurt before sitting down again. 'I was saying to Maxine that of all the places to run into one another——'

'It's amazing,' Kurt cut in, his voice nothing short of jovial. 'Well, Maxine? Am I to take it that you and Mr Lyon are old friends, or what?'

She glared at him. Or what? He knew very well what. She was certain she had mentioned Francis's name to him. Or had she? In any case, he knew who this was all right!

'Maxine and I were once engaged,' Francis said helpfully, looking at her with a smile that showed he felt nothing of the awkwardness she was feeling. 'But it didn't last long, did it?' He turned back to Kurt, shrugging expansively. 'It was just one of those things.'

'One of what things?'

Maxine glared again at the older man but he was not put off; he never was.

'A mistake? Is that what you mean, Mr Lyon?'

He nodded. 'Plain and simple. Still, we found out in time, didn't we, Maxine?'

She had not said anything thus far and she still didn't. She turned to look at Francis with every in-

tention of saying something—something appropriate—but when her eyes caught his, her voice
deserted her. All she could think of was how, *why*,
she had ever got engaged to this man in the first place.
He laughed too loudly, he fancied himself, his sense
of humour was very different from hers and he didn't
take anything seriously. All of which was in evidence
right now.

'Better to find out before tying the knot than after,
eh?' he was saying to Kurt. 'All that unnecessary expense on a wedding...' On that note he laughed again,
obviously thinking himself hilarious.

'Well, there is that,' Kurt conceded with apparent
gravity. 'Followed by all the expense of a divorce. Can
I get you a drink, Mr Lyon? Maxine and I are having
a brandy, how about you?'

Maxine's inward cursing of her boss did nothing to
help; she just wished the floor would open up and
swallow her. She had never known Francis to refuse
a drink and she felt certain he would not refuse this
one.

She was wrong. He looked at his watch and reluctantly shook his head. 'Better not, thanks all the same.
I was about to go to bed when Maxine walked in.'

'So you are staying here?' Kurt said, looking, in
turn, as if he were reluctant to let the younger man
go.

'Yes, I checked in about an hour ago. I stay here
often these days. Well, about once a month, I
suppose.'

'Then why not have a nightcap?'

'Because I'll be on the road again by six in the
morning.'

Politely, Kurt inclined his head, and the fleeting glance he gave Maxine was nothing less than evil—or so it seemed to her.

'So I'll say goodnight,' Francis added, turning to Maxine. 'And it was great seeing you again, you're every bit as gorgeous as I remember you, do you know that?'

'Goodnight, Francis.' Somehow she found her voice—she even managed to put her hand into his when he offered it to her. 'Take care of yourself.'

Kurt waited until Francis was out of sight before speaking. 'By the look of it, I'd better take care of you,' he said, barely able to contain his mirth. 'I'll get you a double.'

She didn't argue; in any case, he was already on his way to the bar. Angrily she stared at his retreating back and prepared to give him a piece of her mind.

As soon as he put their drinks on the table, she took a long swig and almost choked. It was too much for Kurt, he roared with laughter. 'Take it easy, will you? Honestly, if you could see your face! If looks could kill, I'd be——'

'Too right! What the *hell* was all that about?'

'All what?' He sat opposite her, choosing the same chair Francis had sat in. 'Why are you so uptight? What did I do?'

'You embarrassed me, that's what you did. You were being—— '

'I was being myself, which is more than can be said for you. You embarrassed yourself, Maxine, and I'd be very interested to know why. Are you still in love with the man? Why did you feel so awkward? Why did you look so scared?'

'Wait a minute, just wait a minute! I'd like to know why *you* were encouraging him to stay, why you were being so—so hail-fellow-well-met!'

'Why not? Did you expect me to be rude to him?'

'No, of course not. I just...don't understand you,' she finished pathetically.

'Then let me explain,' he said, serious now. 'I was once engaged and I still see my ex-fiancée occasionally. Platonically, of course. Ellen and I are good friends these days——'

If Maxine had been stunned earlier, it was nothing compared to the shock of this. 'You—*what*? Ellen?'

'Ellen Parker. I was engaged to her once and I still see—— '

'All right, all right, I heard you the first time!'

He grunted. 'All I'm trying to point out is that my experience with Ellen did not leave me, or her, in the condition you're in. Evidently, Francis Lyon hasn't been messed up, either, I was glad to see. *He* was behaving naturally—why couldn't you? What is it, Maxine? Are you still in love with him, is that it?'

'Don't be ridiculous!'

'Am I? One could certainly be forgiven for thinking that.'

'I was just shaken up, that's all. Just—surprised to see him. Now leave it, Kurt, I'm going to bed.' She got swiftly to her feet and walked away but Kurt was hard on her heels.

'Just a minute.' As she reached her bedroom door, his hand closed around her wrist. 'I'd like to know what you did feel for Francis just now.'

'Let go of me!' The words came out too harshly and she looked self-consciously along the corridor. Other people were going to their rooms and were glancing interestedly at herself and Kurt.

'Maxine——' With a sigh of impatience he took the key from her hand, opened the door and steered her firmly inside. 'Answer me,' he demanded, uncaring that the door had slammed behind him.

'Get out of here, Kurt. You weren't invited——'

'I said answer me!' Suddenly his hands were on her, their grip on her upper arms almost painful.

'All right, all right! I felt nothing, absolutely nothing except a mild feeling of horror that I might have married him.'

'And where does that leave you now?' He was far too close for comfort and it got worse. He gathered her close to his body, his mouth only inches from hers. 'Maxine?'

'I—don't know what you mean.' When she averted her head he shook her, bringing her eyes back to his. Inwardly she was panicking, her heart was beating too rapidly and she had no idea what he wanted of her, what he expected her to say. 'I really don't know what you mean.'

'Then consider this: you stopped trusting yourself after your mistake with Francis. If the real thing came along right now, you wouldn't recognise it because you're so damned wary, so damned *defended*.'

'Kurt, let go of me——'

He did just the opposite; he pulled her impossibly close, the hard wall of his chest pressing shockingly against her breasts as he brought his mouth down to hers. There was more anger than passion in the kiss, or so it seemed, at least for the first few seconds when she struggled against him.

It was a pointless struggle. It seemed only to inflame him further and in any case his hold on her was vice-like. The protest which tried to escape Maxine's mouth served only to allow him more intimate access to it and Kurt wasted no time in exploring the moist depths with a determined eroticism that provoked a response in her in spite of herself. And then things changed. His mouth became gentle on her, no longer demanding but teasing, almost taunting her to take the initiative now. Which was precisely what she found herself doing. 'Kurt——' The word was spoken against his mouth and she put both hands on the sides of his face, urging him closer as a warm flood of arousal spread rapidly through her body.

It was only when his hand reached to cup the soft contour of her breast that she realised how cleverly he had brought her to this point. Her own hand closed over his, not in invitation but in denial, and Kurt's response to that was both surprising and disappointing. He let go of her at once. 'It's all right, Maxine, you're safe. For tonight at least.'

She looked at him quickly, bemused, doubtful.

'So it's that bad, is it?' He smiled a humourless smile. 'You must want me even more than I'd realised, and you distrust me more than I'd realised. I don't know why, though. I've never given you reason to distrust me.'

'I've never said——' It was as far as she got. She had never said she mistrusted him, but it was true. It was obvious to them both, just as it was now obvious to her that what Kurt wanted was an affair. She stepped away from him, regarding him with open cynicism. 'You're very clever, aren't you? You've told me several times that you expect nothing of me, that you've asked me for nothing.'

'Nor have I.' The brown eyes narrowed in puzzlement. 'So what are you getting at?'

Maxine turned slowly and looked at her bed before answering that one. She gestured towards it, her voice dripping sarcasm as she spoke. 'If I invited you to spend the night with me, you wouldn't refuse.'

'You're too right, I wouldn't!' He was more annoyed than amused; he was looking at her as if she didn't understand anything. 'I want you. I've been perfectly open about that. But I'm not going to coerce you, dammit. I'm not going to *take* anything from you, nor am I going to *ask* or *expect* anything of you. When you come to me,' he added, glancing meaningfully at the bed, 'you will come to me spontaneously and entirely of your own accord. And I'll tell you this, Maxine: it's only a matter of time. As soon as you start trusting yourself again, trusting your own instincts, your knowing of what feels right to you, you'll stop denying us both what we want.'

Then he was gone, leaving Maxine staring after him.

She undressed slowly, hardly noticing what she was doing. Her hands were trembling and her mind was reeling—with resentment at first. Lord, he'd been so sure of himself! Only a matter of time, he'd said, before she stopped denying them both what they wanted. Was he really that confident? Of himself and of her? More importantly, was he right...?

Certainly it had never been like this with Francis. Not with any man had she felt such a strong attraction. In the past it had been so easy, she had never been moved like this before, had never felt——

And was he right? Had she stopped trusting herself, her own judgement? Or had he said that as a ploy, an attempt to undermine her to bring him closer to what he wanted?

Her eyes moved of their own accord towards the wall separating their bedrooms, evoking a vivid imagery to play across her mind. Kurt! Why did it have to be like this with him? Why him, when she had never felt this with any other man? *Was* she falling in love with him? Or was that merely a justification for the sexual desire she felt for him?

CHAPTER SEVEN

MAXINE had more time to think during the following few days. Kurt was no longer interviewing sales reps, which meant their evenings were free, and on the Wednesday she was able to take advantage of the swimming-pool and jacuzzi their hotel proudly boasted.

It had not occurred to her to take a bikini on her travels so she bought one in the hotel's boutique. It was a black and white polka-dot affair, a touch briefer than she would have liked but the shop didn't have a big selection to offer, and when she transferred from the pool to the jacuzzi Kurt was actually the last thing on her mind. She had left him upstairs on the telephone, talking to Jim Ferguson, so it was with a sharp shock that she opened her eyes to see him stepping into the jacuzzi with her. There was only one other person in it, an overweight middle-aged man who appeared to be half asleep.

Kurt flashed her a smile, lowering himself into the teeming blue bubbles directly opposite her. She glanced away, refusing to let her eyes acknowledge openly the strong and solid perfection of his body. It was beautiful, there was no denying that, just as there was no denying her own body's response to the sight of it.

Nothing was said—even when she felt the touch of Kurt's toes against hers in the middle of the spa. She responded by pulling her legs in to break the contact and by closing her eyes. She thought she heard the

124

low rumble of his laughter over the thrum of the
bubbles, but she couldn't be sure. She didn't want to
know if he was laughing; even the idea of it was
enough to ressurect the memory of the way he had
laughed—at her—the previous day...

They had been in this same hotel, in Cardiff, a new
place which had every facility but which hadn't yet
got its act together properly. Their fax machine wasn't
in operation and Kurt had had several to send.

'I'm not going to ask you to go out in this rain,'
he said to Maxine, having been told that faxes could
be sent from a shop further down the road. 'I'll do
it all by telephone instead.'

'That's crazy,' she protested. 'It'll add a fortune to
the hotel bill and I don't mind walking in the rain—
in fact I enjoy it when it isn't windy, which it isn't.
Besides, you wanted some graph paper and I can get
that at the same time.' She stuck out her hand and
smiled. 'Money, please.'

'God!' he said, looking heavenward as if for direct
contact. 'Isn't that just like a woman?'

'There's no use appealing to Him,' she put in
sweetly, 'because it was He who made us all as
delightful as we are.'

Kurt was too busy laughing to retort, and he stuck
his hand in his pocket and fished out some money.
'There you go.'

She got as far as the sitting-room door. 'Will you
be in here when I get back?'

'Where else? I've got about twenty telephone calls
to make in any case.'

'Oh, is that all? Ta-ta, then.' She closed the door
just in time to avoid being hit by a cushion.

When she got back, Kurt told her he had been downstairs to register his complaints. 'I saw the duty manager.'

'Complaints, plural?'

'Complaints numerous, I'll say! There was the fax machine, the cold coffee they delivered here this morning, the frazzled fried eggs on a plate that was as cold as the coffee, the fact that I had to wait seventeen minutes to get an outside line after you'd left, the clogged shower-head in the bathroom and the absence of any hand-towels. Shall I go on?'

'No.' Maxine plonked herself down on the settee facing him, kicking off her shoes at the same time. 'Just tell me how he took the news.'

'With gratitude, of course.'

She grinned from ear to ear. 'Of course.'

'I mean it,' he said, his hands coming up expressively. She hadn't registered, before, how often he did that when he was in earnest. 'It's in his interests to get this place functioning efficiently, so naturally he welcomed my criticisms.'

'Naturally.' Her grin didn't last long. Again a cushion was flung at her and this time it hit target. She threw one back—and the next thing she knew she was lunged at and was having her ribs tickled.

'So! You're ticklish, eh?'

'N-o-o-o! Don't *do* that!' Of course he did, he tickled her mercilessly until she was breathless, breathless one minute and being kissed even more breathless the next. It didn't last long, however, because Kurt put her firmly away from him.

'Maxine——'

'I know. I—that wasn't my fault.'

It was then that he'd laughed at her. 'There's no "fault" involved. It's just that you're becoming more

than I'm able to resist.' The laughter had faded at
that point. 'And I'm warning you fair and square,
Maxine ... if you give me an inch, I shall take a mile.'

Now, she looked at him across the bubbling water
and found that his gaze was fixed firmly on her. For
seconds she held it, feeling an unprecedented surge of
desire for him. More than he was able to resist? The
same thing was happening to her, too, and she began
to wonder why she was continuing to resist. Why not
give in to her desires, why not flow with them, simply
allow them?

Again she closed her eyes, cutting off the blatant
message she could see in his. A moment later she got
out of the water, feeling acutely self-conscious because Kurt's eyes were still on her, almost caressing
her as she climbed the steps. The eroticism, from the
male point of view, of her retreating bottom in the
skimpy bikini did not escape her. She was still pink
in the face by the time she reached their suite of rooms.

She got straight into the shower and soaped herself
almost frantically, as if to wash away not the desire
she felt but the doubts she knew. What was it about
Kurt that she didn't trust? What was this niggling
doubt about him which lurked in the recesses of her
mind? As he had pointed out, he had given her no
reason to mistrust him—yet she did.

Suddenly her hands stilled and she stood motionless, realising how unfounded her distrust was. She
was being paranoid, that was all. Kurt had been right
in pointing out to her that it was *herself* she didn't
trust, that it was her own judgement she had ceased
to rely on.

She switched off the shower and wrapped a towel
around her, feeling grateful now for the coincidence
which had placed her and Francis Lyon in the same

hotel a few days ago. She knew now that if ever she should meet Francis again she would behave very differently, without any awkwardness or discomfiture. Never again would seeing him, or thinking of him, serve only as a reminder of a mistake. In thinking of it as such, all she had actually succeeded in doing was colouring negatively her outlook on men, all men, and in particular her attitude towards emotional involvement. That outlook had in effect been a self-punishment—and for what? For something that had been an illusion, not just her supposed love for Francis but also the way she had allowed it to affect her.

A wry smile touched her lips at the memory of Kurt asking her whether she intended to live like a nun. No, she didn't intend that. But she did not intend either to have the string of affairs he had obviously had in his life. That might be Kurt's style but it wasn't hers . . . and *that* was the reason for her holding back. It wasn't that she mistrusted him, it was the feeling that it wouldn't mean anything to him if she did go to bed with him. Would it? Would it mean anything? Anything at all?

'Maxine? Are you in there?'

At the sound of his voice outside the bathroom door, an illogical flash of anger shot through her. It was probably due to the thought she'd just had, her assumption that she would be just another conquest to Kurt. She didn't stop to think, then, that his interest in her went further than her body, that if she meant nothing more than that to him he wouldn't *care* about the hang-ups she'd had.

'Of course I'm in here.' Her voice reflected her anger, more so than she realised, and when she opened the door and tried to walk past Kurt he caught hold of her arm and stopped her.

'Hey! What's the matter with you? It was a civil question, wasn't it? I only want to take a shower.'

'I—yes, I'm sorry.' She hardly knew where to look. Clad only in a towel, barefoot as she was, her face came level with his throat—but she was shockingly aware of every inch of him. Over the brief trunks he'd worn in the jacuzzi there was just a towelling robe— open almost to the waist—which did nothing to dull the memory of his near-nakedness. 'Sorry,' she repeated, feeling idiotic now.

'What is the matter with you?' The grip on her arm tightened, bringing her eyes up to his. She saw impatience in them. 'What dark thoughts are you harbouring against me now, Maxine?'

'None. You just startled me, that's all.' Again she made a move to get away from him and again his grip tightened, bringing her illogical anger back in a flash. 'Kurt, let go of me!'

'I'll let go when you tell me what I've done—what is it this time?' He hauled her closer, his eyes searching hers in genuine puzzlement. Then, suddenly, he was smiling, giving her no warning of his intention other than a softly muttered, 'I see...'

There was no time to wonder what he had seen, or what conclusions he had jumped to, because his mouth was on hers and he was kissing her as if kissing were about to go out of fashion.

Maxine put both hands flat on his chest and tried, and failed, to create a space between their bodies. She also tried to get over the moment by being flippant. 'Tell me, Mr Raynor, do you do this with all your secretaries?'

'No.' He wasn't smiling; his eyes were still on her mouth.

'So you wouldn't be doing this if Linda Storton were standing here instead of me?'

That made him laugh. He threw back his head and roared. 'Linda? My dear lovely Maxine, Linda Storton is a darling—but she's also old enough to be my mother!'

'Oh!' Now she really felt idiotic. For some reason, she had taken it for granted that Linda would be around her own age. 'Well, I . . . will you let go of me now, please? I want to get dressed.'

With a knowing smile he did as she asked, and Maxine froze on the spot. The towel she had so carefully wrapped around her had come untied and it slipped to the floor the instant Kurt moved from her.

Only for one second did their eyes meet before she found herself watching his gaze moving steadily, slowly, down the entire length of her body, naked and immobile as it was, as if it had a mind of its own, as if *it* refused to move. She saw his arm lifting, she felt the gentle touch of his fingers as he cupped her breast, and still she couldn't move. 'Kurt——'

'Ssshh!' The urgency in the sound silenced her. That, and the way he was looking at her with such appreciation, almost a wonderment. Her name came to his lips almost inaudibly as his other hand reached out to touch her, his thumbs brushing lightly over the pink tips of her breasts, already taut and straining towards the contact. 'Maxine . . . you're so beautiful! So beautiful . . .'

Her brain jerked into action. She grasped his wrists and pushed his hands away, hoping against hope that he would be as good as his word and not push things. For reasons she still could not fathom fully, she was not ready for this—not yet. 'I'm going out.' She almost shouted the words, ignoring his unconcealed bewilderment. 'I'm not eating with you tonight, I'm going out to do my own thing.'

With that, she scooped up her towel and bolted. It would not have surprised her had the sound of his laughter followed as she stepped into her bedroom, but it didn't. There was only a regretful, 'As you wish, Maxine, as you wish.'

Their hotel room in Bournemouth overlooked the sea and the view from Maxine's bedroom was pretty. She stood looking at it on the Thursday evening, watching the twinkle of lights along the bay. It was her birthday and she was feeling blue; she had not managed to catch Polly when she'd phoned home that morning, and this was her first experience of having a birthday pass apparently unnoticed.

She turned from the window and lay on the bed, exhausted. It had been a crazy, hectic day which had included the long drive from Cardiff, and although she was hungry the prospect of making up and dressing up was too much. She had been grateful to get out of her clothes an hour ago, to take a bath and relax at last. She would eat up here tonight, tell Kurt to go ahead and have dinner in the restaurant without her. He had booked a table for eight o'clock. She let her eyes close, listening to the muffled sound of his voice from the sitting-room. He was on the telephone; he had been making calls from the time they'd booked in to the hotel.

'Maxine?' Her eyes came open at the sound of his voice. 'Are you decent?'

She was decent enough, clad in the satin dressing-gown he'd seen her in often before. 'Come in.'

He opened her bedroom door and stuck his head round it. 'I'm about to shower, I'll be ready in fifteen minutes, OK?'

'No.' She shook her head. 'I'm feeling lazy tonight, Kurt. You go down when you're ready, I just can't be bothered dressing, so I'm going to order from room service.'

He smiled. 'I can understand that. Today was a bit mad, wasn't it? And it's funny, because I'd thought of suggesting we ate in the sitting-room tonight.' It was not what she'd had in mind, she would rather be alone for a while, but what could she say? Especially when Kurt added, 'I'm quite shattered myself.'

'Fine, so we'll both eat up here.' She closed her eyes again and fell asleep without intending to. The next thing she heard was the sound of Kurt calling her name. Tiredly she went into the sitting-room to join him. It was a spacious, airy room with another view of the sea—not that she could see it now because Kurt had closed the curtains against the darkness. All the lamps were on—there was no overhead light, just lamps and spotlights over the paintings on the walls.

He had lowered his big frame into an armchair and was watching her closely, his feet resting on the low coffee-table that stood between them. 'Why don't we have a drink?'

Maxine shrugged. 'If you like. Give me a few minutes, I'll throw some clothes on.'

'Why bother? I thought you wanted to relax.'

She glanced at him a little warily, remembering very well the warning he had given her about the inch and the mile. 'I will be relaxed.' She hoped it was the truth, although Kurt looked too attractive for her to be totally at ease, dressed as he was in black trousers and sweater, his hair still damp from his shower, combed back from his forehead, looking darker than it actually was.

When she joined him again, his eyes travelled over her rapidly and dismissed her. She was glad of their lack of interest; she had changed quite deliberately into a lounging suit that could hardly be more unflattering to her figure. She hadn't worn it before—there had been no time for lounging—and it was baggy on her, a cross between pyjamas and a tracksuit. The only attractive thing about it was the soft, pale pink material it was made of.

'I just ordered from room service,' he told her. 'They'll bring dinner at eight-thirty, OK?'

He had ordered without asking her what she wanted to eat? 'Fine.' She was not going to make an issue of it; she didn't care enough. Instead she watched him as he crossed the sitting-room. There was a mini-bar in here, in the form of a refrigerator that looked like a piece of furniture. 'I'll have a gin and tonic, please, if there is some.'

Kurt nodded. 'There's everything from beer to champagne in here. And,' he added, glancing over at her, 'since it's your birthday, champagne is what we'll have.'

Feeling ridiculously pleased, Maxine laughed in pure delight. She had thought he had no idea—and she would never have mentioned it. Her blues suddenly lifted, for she had assumed her birthday would pass uncelebrated. 'How did you know?'

'That you've reached the grand old age of twenty-four today? Someone told me.' The cork on the bottle went pop and a moment later he was handing her a glass of bubbling wine. 'Here's to you, Maxine. Happy birthday!'

She raised her glass, smiling back at him. 'Who told you?'

'Actually, it was a little——'

'Oh, *Kurt*! Don't say a little bird! Tell me, I'm curious.'

'I'll do better than that, I'll show you.' And with that he put his glass down and went into his bedroom. Maxine was still laughing—a moment's thought had provided the answer: Kurt had looked over all his staff's personnel records.

A few seconds later he was back with a box, about a foot square, gift-wrapped in gold paper and tied with a bright red ribbon.

Maxine's pleasure was childlike as she looked from him to the box and back again. 'That's—for me?'

He laughed, placing the box ceremoniously on the coffee-table in front of her. 'What do you think? Well, aren't you going to open it?'

'You bet!' She opened the box without ceremony, eagerly tossing the wrapping aside. For a moment she couldn't speak; tears threatened because she was so touched, very touched. In the box was the little lamb, or an exact replica of it, which she had seen in the window of the shop in Betws-y-Coed last Sunday. 'Oh, Kurt . . . he's lovely!'

'Now how do you know it's a he?' Kurt picked up his champagne and sat next to her on the settee. 'Do you know something I don't? Actually, it isn't the one you saw, this is his cousin who lives—used to live— in Swansea.'

'His cousin?' She turned to him, her eyes glowing.

'Mm. And *he* told me it was your birthday today.'

'Oh, you are an idiot! Thank you, I love him!'

'Lucky him,' he said with an exaggerated sigh. 'Some lambs have all the luck. And what do I get?'

He got a kiss on the cheek, and still he grumbled. 'Is that all?'

'That's all.' It was supposed to come out sternly but she was unable to hold back a new burst of laughter.

'Ah, well.' Kurt fished in his pocket. From it he took a box covered in dark blue velvet. 'Let's see if I'll have any more luck with this.'

Maxine's smile faded. What now? 'Kurt——'

'It's only a trinket, just a thank-you for your efforts, that's all.'

The 'trinket' was a long, chunky, solid gold chain. 'Oh, no, I—I can't accept that!'

'Yes, you can.'

'Kurt, no, it's too much, it's——'

'I told you, it's just my way of saying thank you for a job well done. Now enough, I don't want any more argument.' He took the chain from the box and held it up. 'Come here, come closer.' He put the chain in place around her neck, lifting her hair out of the way and letting his fingers linger in it. 'Well, Maxine?'

She did not give herself time to think; she slid her arms around him and kissed him on the mouth, feeling his body stiffen before she let go. 'Thank you, it's beautiful.'

'So are you . . .' Then it was he who was kissing her, pulling her back into his arms, his kiss deepening as his tongue began a much longed for re-exploration. It was also he who called a halt, and when he raised his head it was Maxine who was breathless, flushed, feeling unsatisfied. She had wanted to stay in his arms but he was moving from her, going back to the armchair facing her.

'Kurt . . . ?'

He smiled, but there was no humour in it. 'Leave it, birthday girl. I want this to be a nice evening and I've told you how it is with me; I don't need any encouragement. I'm aching for you, Maxine. Right now. I'll make no bones about it.'

She almost shivered, his words both exciting and alarming her at the same time. If he were seriously to set about seducing her she would, she knew, have no chance. She wouldn't be able to make a detached, conscious decision; she would be putty in his hands. She tore her eyes away from his and looked down at the carpet, going on to wonder if perhaps that was the way she wanted it, in her heart of hearts.

Her thinking was interrupted by a sharp knock on the door, a voice informing them it was room service.

'I'll get it.' Kurt was on his feet in a flash, crossing the room with his light, graceful tread.

'Good evening, sir. Madam.' A table was wheeled in, covered with a crisp white cloth on which there were several silver dishes with high domes. The waiter was grinning almost smugly, as if he knew something the rest of the world didn't know.

Maxine watched him as he set out cutlery and napkins with a flourish—and then she realised how accurate her observation had been. On the bottom section of the table, visible where the cloth ended, was a birthday cake, beautifully, intricately decorated, complete with icing that read, 'Happy Birthday, Maxine!'

Her eyes flew from the cake to Kurt. He had planned this all along! He had booked a table in the restaurant for eight o'clock—he had been going to spring this surprise on her there. She was and was not sorry she had wrought a change in his plan; being presented with a birthday cake in public would have made her very self-conscious. Oh, but what a generous thought! She blew a kiss at him, wishing the waiter would hurry up and leave.

He did, but not before he had lifted all the domes to show her what she would be eating. Kurt had got it just right, all the dishes she favoured, the main course being chateaubriand with tiny roast potatoes and buttered carrots. He must have been making notes this past fortnight, watching what she ordered!

The moment they were alone she thanked him, laughing and flinging her arms around him. 'This is very kind of you. Honestly, you make me feel like a little girl. Woolly lambs and birthday cakes——'

'I do?' He looked down at her, his arms tightening as he held her body against him. 'Then I've done something wrong, somewhere.' His hold on her tightened until she could feel every contour of him, the warm pressure of every muscle. He nuzzled his face in her hair, his lips against her ear. 'Still feel like a little girl?'

Maxine laughed up at him. 'The food, dear man. Let's *eat*!'

It was more than just dinner, it was a feast, during which Kurt opened a second bottle of champagne as they ploughed their way through several courses, drinking and talking about things she couldn't remember later—except that they exchanged some jokes and a lot of laughter.

She had been giggling anyway—and not minding in the least. So what if she was giggling? She was happy, happier than she could remember being in a long time. At length Kurt got up to put the radio on— or rather the piped music which was of a kind that could offend no one—and asked her to dance.

'Not a chance!' She stayed where she was, laughing at him. It was just as well she was wearing what she was wearing—there was room for expansion! 'I couldn't move if I wanted to.'

But she did, when the waiter came to remove the table, bringing with him a tray set with cups and a pot of steaming coffee—with a plate of delicate little chocolates and marzipans. He placed the tray carefully on the coffee-table before retreating.

'Kurt, come here.' Maxine patted the cushion next to her. 'You'll have to pour. I tell you, I haven't even got the energy to lift that pot.'

'At your service, madam.'

Ten minutes later he slipped his arm around her shoulders and, as if it were the most natural thing in the world, Maxine rested her head against his chest, content just to sit in silence. She noticed that the lamb was now occupying the armchair and the birthday cake had been relegated to the top of the fridge, untouched.

'What are you thinking?' he asked, his voice a soft breeze against her hair.

'I'm not thinking.'

'Befuddled from the champagne?'

'Yes,' she admitted. She was tipsy, decidedly tipsy.

'Hey, you're not going to fall asleep on me, are you? We haven't had any birthday cake yet; we've got to light that candle—and you have to make a wish!'

'I suppose so... but just the tiniest piece, Kurt.'

When the candle on the cake was lit, Maxine hesitated before blowing it out. What to wish for? Her eyes went to Kurt. No, that was too much to wish for! In any case, why wish he felt the same way about her as she did about him when she wasn't sure *what* she felt for him, not exactly?

'Maxine? What is it? Why are you looking at me like that?'

'Sorry, I—I have several wishes, I was just trying to decide on which one.'

'You only get the one,' he smiled. 'So wish wisely, my lovely.'

She did not in fact wish for anything, but she didn't let Kurt know that. She cut the cake and, a short time later, a little bleep from his watch told her that another hour had passed. 'What time is that?'

'Eleven.'

'Eleven? Already? I must make a move...' It was work as usual in the morning.

His arm came around her shoulders. 'Stay around for another hour,' he coaxed. 'Let's see your birthday out.'

The stillness stopped her from moving, from saying anything. His stillness. Hers. Their eyes had met and held and, suddenly, he was kissing her. It didn't cross her mind to stop him; she wanted it too much. Her arms went around him automatically, and when he eased her body back against the settee she yielded willingly.

'Maxine...' Kurt's lips were at her throat, at the side of her neck, the lobes of her ears. He shifted his weight so he was stretched out alongside her, his body partly covering hers with a welcome, satisfying weight.

'Kurt...' It was half murmur, half groan. Again and again she mindlessly said his name as his mouth blazed a trail of fire across her skin. When at last it came back to claim her mouth, her hunger was such that she kissed him in a way that she had never kissed him before, never kissed anyone before. She could not get enough of him. She gave herself up to his exploration, shivering when the pressure of it lightened, when his tongue ran along the inside of her lips before plunging deeply, deeply, suggesting, demanding, promising...

In her mind she was already making love with him and she could think of nothing but that, of stretching out with him on the bed and being one with him. When his hand slipped beneath her top to cover her breast, she arched against him involuntarily. A small gasp tried to free itself but it was stifled against the pressure of his mouth.

Kurt reacted to it with a groan, lifting his head so he could plant kisses, little kisses, over her face, lightly and with tenderness, on her lips, her nose, her cheeks, her closed eyelids. 'Dear lord, I want you—how I want you, Maxine!'

Maxine heard the words but she was beyond thought now, she was no longer in the immediate future, imagining herself already in bed with Kurt, she was wholly in the present, able to register only what was happening to her body this minute. She felt his hands easing the top of her suit away from her breasts, followed by the shocking, unbelievable ecstasy that was his mouth on them, sucking and taunting. The near roughness of his hands there served only to inflame her further and this time she cried out. Then one hand was on her thigh, moving slowly upwards until she felt the caress of his fingers on that most intimate part of her. And still there was no resistance, there was only the unashamed encouragement of a woman hungry to know the deepest fulfilment. With everything in her she urged him on, with her mouth, with her body, with the sensual little noises she wasn't even aware she was making.

How many times the telephone had already trilled, she had no idea, for that was another noise she was not aware of—not at first. When she eventually heard it, it came dimly, as if from a great distance. She stirred but Kurt held her. 'Leave it.'

It persisted. It seemed to be getting louder. 'Kurt——'

'Ignore it!' His breathing was laboured, his body tense with its need of her. But Maxine's mind was clearing, enough to make her realise quite how far things had gone. How far gone Kurt was. As if to prove it he moved, just slightly, so that the force of his desire was communicated unmistakably.

And still the trilling got louder. 'Kurt, the phone. It might be . . . something must be wrong. Kurt!'

He pulled away, his fingers savagely raking the hair from his forehead. He attempted to nod, to say something, while Maxine thought with shock that she had never seen such a look on his face. He seemed to be in pain.

Quickly she got up, crossing the room rapidly to pick up the phone on the writing bureau near the window. 'Hello?'

'Maxine? Hi! Happy birthday!'

'Polly!' She glanced over at Kurt, a look of apology on her face. What she saw on his face made her turn her back to him again; he looked stunned, as if he wasn't sure what was happening.

'Why so surprised?' her sister was saying. 'I would have phoned earlier but I've been out. Just got in, in time to wish you many happy returns before midnight. Maxine? Are you still there?'

'I'm—yes. Thank you, Polly.'

'Is something wrong? Oh, dear! Were you in bed? Did I wake you?'

For an instant, the comedy of the situation struck Maxine. She wondered what Kurt might be thinking, that this was some elaborate, impossible conspiracy on her part, or hers and Polly's? 'No,' she said, trying hard to steady her voice, 'I wasn't in bed.' She bit her lip. Not in bed, not in bed. But if Polly hadn't phoned...if she had phoned just a little later...

'Well, I didn't think you would be,' Polly went on. 'I thought you'd have been celebrating.'

'I—was.'

There was a groan, a near audible penny dropping. 'Oh, hell! I've interrupted something, haven't I?'

'No, no, not at all.'

'Come on, I'm your sister, remember? Look, I'm sorry, Max, I'll ring off. See you on Saturday.'

The line went dead and Maxine stood motionless for a moment, the receiver still in her hand. Even as she stood, she could feel Kurt's eyes on her back, and it was slowly that she turned around to face him. 'It—was Polly,' she said needlessly.

'She certainly picked her moment.' He was not amused, not in the least. If there was any humour in the situation, he was in no condition to see it. He came over to her, put his hands on her shoulders and held her against him.

'You mustn't blame Polly,' she said dully. 'She only wanted to say happy birthday before the day was out.'

'I know.' He sighed, long and deep, before cupping her chin in his hands. 'Come on, let's go to bed. And if perchance the phone should ring again——' He broke off. Maxine was shaking her head and there was disbelief on his face. *'No?'*

'No, Kurt. The moment has passed, and you know it.'

He smiled at that, bending to kiss her closed mouth very lightly. 'We can recreate it. I assure you, that will be no problem at all.'

'No.' She couldn't, because for her the moment had passed and the ill-timed interruption had allowed those nebulous doubts to come back.

'Maxine——' A note of annoyance crept into his voice. 'Darling, listen to me.' But he didn't give her anything to listen to. Instead he kissed her, not lightly but forcefully, so much so that his lips were bruising against hers.

She twisted her head free. 'Kurt, I said no. It's too late.'

'Too late? What kind of late?' he demanded. 'Late because it's eleven-thirty or late because you've changed your mind? Well, I'm not going to allow you to do that, Maxine. We've come this far, we've——'

'Allow it?' That was all she had heard. '*Allow* it? What the hell is that supposed to mean?'

He was trying to be patient with her, she knew that, but his anger was showing through unmistakably. 'It means we've gone too far to stop now and I'm damned if we're going to.'

'I see!' Suddenly she did see. She saw it all. Why she hadn't realised earlier, she would never know, but it was very clear now that this entire evening had been planned by him from start to finish! The gifts, the cake, the champagne, the dinner. His so-called thoughtfulness. The little things over which she had felt so touched. It had just been a seduction routine, a way of wearing her down where words had failed. Kurt himself would be the first to admit that when words were inadequate other solutions should be sought. He had known precisely what to do and she had made it easier for him by wanting to eat in here! She almost laughed at the irony of that—until she realised that that, too, had been planned very neatly. He'd only *said* he'd booked a table in the restaurant.

It was true that eating in their rooms had been her suggestion, but he'd said that he was going to suggest it, too—apparently as a last-minute change of mind!

'Maxine?' He caught hold of her, clearly alarmed by the look in her eyes. 'Maxine, for heaven's sake——'

'For heaven's sake what?' She was perfectly calm, for the moment. It wouldn't last, she knew full well that once she reached the safety of her room she would cry. She was an idiot, a naïve idiot. Compared to this man, with all his experience, she was a total innocent. 'What, Kurt? For heaven's sake, how can I do this? For heaven's sake, don't I know how much you want me? Yes, I know. I know you planned this evening very elaborately! You knew precisely how to soften me up—right through to the second bottle of champagne and finally to coaxing me to stick around till midnight. I'll say this for you, when it comes to being devious you're a past master. I wonder——'

'No!' He caught hold of her, shaking her. 'No, you're absolutely wrong!'

'I wonder,' she went on, in spite of his shaking her, 'with how many women, in how many hotel rooms you've gone through this routine. I wonder——' She felt and heard her voice crack. If she didn't get away from him, rapidly, she was going to break down and cry like a baby. Anger towards herself almost choked her—but it was nothing compared to her anger with him. It gave her the strength to wrench free, to flee to the safety of her room. But there was time enough for her to register the shock on his face as she turned away, time enough to see the curious mixture of disbelief, sadness and anger all at the same time. For once in her experience he was speechless, looking more vulnerable than she'd ever seen him.

CHAPTER EIGHT

THE last leg of their journey home was awful. They had not been due to go back until Saturday and today was Friday, but Kurt had announced that once the morning's business had been dealt with they were heading home. He'd had enough, he'd said, with a meaningful look at her across the breakfast table.

That had been an excruciating forty minutes during which they had both wanted to say a great deal—but nothing had been said. Maxine had not cried the previous night; the look she had seen on Kurt's face as she wrenched away from him had haunted her, making her realise how she had over-reacted. Had she accused him wrongly? After all, she had given him every possible encouragement and, perverse though it seemed even to herself, she wished now that the telephone had never rung, that things had continued to happen as she had, in that moment, wanted them to happen.

She glanced surreptitiously at Kurt, whose eyes were firmly on the road. They had set off driving in silence and had spoken no more than a dozen words to one another since. Whether he had deliberately planned a seduction scenario last night hardly mattered now. What mattered was the present situation. Where did they go from here? He was her employer, she had managed to forget that—but how could she go on working for him now? And yet...the idea of handing in her notice was an unwelcome one.

If only she could talk to him, really talk. If only she knew what she actually wanted to say. That would help, she thought wryly, still wondering what it was that held her back. Maybe she should listen to her heart rather than her head, because the doubts were all in her mind, surely, whatever they were.

Again she glanced at him through the invisible wall separating them, unsure whether or not he had just said something.

He had. 'Maxine, I just asked you if you'd like to stop for a cup of coffee.'

'No, thank you, I'd like to press on. I'll have a lot to do when I get home.'

By the time they reached the outskirts of Oldfield it was late afternoon and Maxine had never been so relieved to see the village where she had lived all her life. Kurt stopped the Rolls at the bottom of her drive, got out and took her case from the boot. 'One suitcase and one secretary delivered safe and sound.' He wasn't smiling, he wasn't even looking at her, and his parting words came as a disappointment and a relief at the same time. 'I'll be in the office on Monday morning to talk to Jim, sort out the orders we've taken, after which you'll see little of me. At lunchtime I'll be going over to Watford and that's where I'll be for the rest of the week.'

'Right.' Maxine picked up her case and he let her go without another word.

She opened the front door, dropped her case to the floor and found herself promptly bursting into tears. Blindly she walked to the kitchen and filled the kettle, acknowledging at last what was really troubling her. She was in love with him. There was no longer any room for doubt.

But what the devil was she going to *do*?

As soon as she came face to face with her sister that evening, she was weeping again and the whole story came pouring out of her with enormous relief. 'I very nearly went to bed with him last night,' she said at length. 'And this morning, I wished I had.'

Polly smiled. 'Well, that's easily remedied.'

'I know, but it's too late now.'

'What do you mean?'

'I mean I'm in love with him. I've been denying it to myself, right up until I got home this afternoon. But——' she shrugged '—there it is.'

There was a groan, an understanding nod. 'And you don't think he feels the same way?'

'I know he doesn't. All he wants is an affair.'

'Max, are you sure about that? I mean——' She was interrupted by the ringing of the doorbell. 'That'll be David.'

It was seven-thirty according to the clock on the mantel. The weekend starts here, Maxine thought unhappily. And it was going to feel like a long one unless she could find some means of distracting herself. Perhaps David would be staying here, perhaps the three of them could go out together.

No.

Then maybe she would go to the orphanage tomorrow. They weren't expecting her because she hadn't been due home until tomorrow evening, but still . . .

No.

'Maxine? Hi. Happy birthday for yesterday.' Her prospective brother-in-law handed her a gift and during the next hour or so managed, simply by chatting, to take her mind off her immediate problem.

By the time he and Polly were ready to go out for the evening, the problem seemed to have solved itself. She would hand in her notice on Monday.

'You're sure you won't come out with us, Max?'
There was sympathetic understanding in Polly's eyes—
and concern.

Maxine saw the concern and brightened. 'No,
thanks. I'm all right. I've decided to hand in my notice
on Monday.'

There was a questioning look from David, promptly
defused by Polly with, 'I'll explain to you later.'

The sheer luxury of sleeping till noon was something
Maxine enjoyed only rarely. It was ten minutes to
twelve when she woke and two o'clock by the time
she'd had some tea and had showered and dressed.
Polly had left a note saying she was going to London
for the day with David.

At two fifteen the doorbell rang.

Chiding herself for hoping it would be Kurt, she
had to school her features into a pleasant smile for
William Harrison. 'William, what a nice surprise! Do
come in.'

He was beaming, obviously pleased to see her. The
first thing he told her was that he'd missed her. 'I
didn't know what time you'd be getting back but I
just saw Kurt in the village, so I realised——'

'Kurt?'

William glanced over his shoulder as he preceded
her into the living-room, frowning. 'Your boss, of
course. He was in Lawley's tea shop and he introduced me to that gorgeous blonde of his, Ellen
Parker.'

'What——' The sentence snapped off before it got
under way. William didn't seem to notice. Nor did he
notice how very still Maxine went. He was sitting
himself down and she had frozen on the spot.

Ellen Parker?

But—that was the name of the woman Kurt had been *engaged* to! He'd mentioned her name and...
'William, are you talking about the same blonde we saw with Kurt in the Copper Kettle that night?'

'Of course. Why? How many has he got?' This was followed with laughter which Maxine forced herself to share, while inwardly she started to boil.

Kurt Raynor was a *rat*! So she had *not* been mistaken about his seduction routine last Thursday, and all she could do now was thank heaven she had resisted. Thank heaven—and thank Polly for her timely interruption.

'I still see my ex-fiancée occasionally.' Kurt's words came back to her like a recurring nightmare. 'Platonically, of course. Ellen and I are good friends these days...'

In a pig's eye! There was no way on this earth that Kurt's relationship with Ellen Parker was platonic. The memory of them together was all too clear to Maxine and all the signals of a sexual relationship had been unmistakably there. She might have chosen to forget that during this past fortnight—but she wasn't able to forget it now.

'Maxine? Are you feeling all right? You've gone pale.'

'I'm fine, thank you, Doctor.' Somehow she managed to smile. Somehow she managed to remember her manners and offer him a cup of tea. And, somehow, she managed to look enthusiastic when she accepted his invitation out that evening.

Going to the office on Monday was not something Maxine had been looking forward to. She arrived at nine sharp to see Kurt sitting behind his desk, in conference with the warehouse manager, the factory foreman and Jim Ferguson. She saw them through the glass partition as she hung up her coat. Kurt glanced up but he did not beckon her in, which of itself was strange because she should have been in on that meeting.

She shrugged inwardly. If he didn't want her there, he didn't want her there; it gave her the perfect opportunity to type her letter of resignation. With luck she would see very little of him between now and the day she left—he had said he would be in Watford all week, and she hoped he would spend most of the following week there, too.

It was almost lunchtime before the meeting broke up in the next office. Maxine had got on with the routine work for Jim after putting her letter of resignation in an envelope; all she had to do now was wait for her opportunity to hand it over.

'Maxine, hello there! Nice to have you back.' Jim breezed in eventually, shirt-sleeves rolled up, tie loose at his neck, as usual. 'Well, you two certainly did us proud this past couple of weeks! We've got enough orders to—is something wrong?'

'No, I—well, sort of. Er—please excuse me, Jim, I must have a word with Kurt.'

'You've just missed him.' The boss had moved over to the window overlooking the car park, and the big boss, it seemed, had just driven away, without a word to her, not a single word!

'But—dammit!' The word burst from her. Damn the man, he hadn't even said as much as good morning. And now he was gone—gone before she had handed over her resignation. She clenched her fists in frustration, thumping them on her desk.

Jim's eyebrows shot up. 'Hey, hey, hey! What gives? This isn't my cool, level-headed secretary, this isn't the even-tempered girl I last saw two weeks ago. What has that man done to you?'

'I'm sorry,' she said quickly. This had nothing to do with Jim. He was right—as far as he was concerned she was cool and level-headed. She couldn't tell him, she couldn't tell Jim Ferguson anything; he and Kurt were friends of many years.

She put both hands flat on her desk and struggled for composure. 'Jim, I typed out a letter of resignation this morning. I intended to give it to Kurt before he left for Watford.'

There was a long silence during which the boss looked at her very carefully, his eyes narrowing before he pulled a chair up to her desk. 'Tell me,' he said quietly. 'What's been going on?'

'Nothing. I'm just—leaving.'

'Just like that? Without a reason?'

'Oh, of course there's a reason,' she said casually, as if he were being silly. 'Obviously I've thought this through carefully. You see, it's just that I've decided to look for a job in London, something with better prospects.'

'There are prospects here, Maxine. When you work for Kurt Raynor there are always prospects, and no one is better than he at judging people, judging their potential. If you have it in mind to take on added responsibility, to move up in your career, you're already at the right place.'

'Well, you see, it isn't just that. I—I really need to look for something with a better salary.'

'What? After the fat rise Kurt gave you a couple of weeks ago? Do you think that's reasonable?'

'He did? I hadn't realised.'

'Surely you discussed it with him?' Jim looked puzzled, as well he might.

Maxine had discussed it with Kurt, the Friday before they had left for their trip, she had told him how much extra she wanted—and now Jim was telling her he had doubled it!

'He told me over the phone a couple of Mondays ago, when you were in Aberdeen. So that's that!' he added cheerfully, convinced he had now removed Maxine's reason for wanting to leave.

She knew she was scraping the barrel with her next protest; she thought she might get away with it because Jim would not pry. She was wrong. 'Actually, it's the hours I put in here, Jim, they're interfering with my evening classes and——'

'And if you were commuting from London every evening, they wouldn't? Maxine, do me a favour, just tell me what's really bothering you.'

What could she say? He had destroyed her excuses with such ease, and she couldn't think of any more. 'It's—well, Kurt and I don't get on, that's the top and bottom of it.'

'And you,' Jim said bluntly, 'are lying through your teeth. I've never heard such codswallop in all my life. Kurt might have got under your skin, but not because you can't get on with him. I suspect you've been getting on very well indeed this past couple of weeks— in fact, I know you have.'

Maxine glared at him. What on earth had Kurt told him? 'What's that supposed to mean?'

'Relax!' He laughed at her, shaking his head at the same time. 'It means Kurt told me so in as many words, that's all. You must bear in mind that I've spoken to him on the phone every day and he's been singing your praises very loudly. So try again—or better still, save time and tell me the truth.'

'Jim, I——' Oh, lord! She felt cornered; he was not going to let her off the hook. There was only one avenue of escape left open to her and, given that she would be leaving soon, it would make no difference to anyone if she took it. So she got angry, fast. 'This really is none of your business! All you need to know is that I'm leaving in two weeks' time!'

For several seconds nothing was said. Then Jim nodded reluctantly. 'If you insist. But, Maxine, please do me a favour—I mean me, personally. Make it four weeks' notice, would you? I've only just settled in here myself—I don't want to have to train someone new to the business.'

'But there's Denise——'

'No. With all due respect, she's not up to this job on a permanent basis. Let's find someone, then if you'll stay on just long enough to break her in—a month should do it. Two weeks just isn't enough. Please, Maxine.'

Her mouth opened and closed. She did not want to be unreasonable, two weeks' notice was as much as she needed to give officially, but . . . Jim was such a nice man. 'I'll compromise,' she said at length. 'Three weeks. That will take us to Easter and I'm going on holiday then in any case.'

'So you are. I'd forgotten.'

'I'll finish on the day before Good Friday.' Which meant she would have to have everything ready to pack that evening. She and Polly were leaving for France on Good Friday morning.

'All right—done!' The boss looked relieved, which made her feel guilty. 'I suppose you'd better alter that,' he said, glancing at the envelope in her hand. 'Then give it to me. I'll put it in my desk drawer and I'll give it to Kurt tonight. He'll be calling in on his way home—long after you've gone, I dare say. If you are still here, well, you know where it is. I'll leave it in the top drawer then you can do the dirty deed yourself.'

Maxine sighed. 'I'm sorry you feel like that, Jim, but this is how it has to be, believe me. And I'm sorry I snapped at you.'

'I'm sorry too,' he said, with no sign of having taken offence. 'I have just one thing to say, Maxine,' he added, with a reassuring smile. 'I know Kurt Raynor extremely well and...'

'And what?'

'That wasn't what I intended to say at all. What I want to say is that if ever you feel like talking to me, about anything at all, please don't hesitate. I like you, Maxine, you and Kurt are both super people in my book.'

She said something trite in answer, something evasive, something she couldn't even remember that evening, when she finally had some time alone with her sister.

They were in Maxine's bedroom; she was getting dressed for another date with William Harrison and she was ranting at the same time—about Ellen Parker.

Polly had already heard about it that morning. She had not been convinced that Maxine had definite grounds for her anger, and she was still unsure. 'But it *might* be platonic, Max. Stranger things have happened——'

'Do me a favour! You should *see* the woman, she oozes sex appeal, she just oozes it!'

'Nevertheless...' Polly shrugged. 'Is this why you're taking up with William Harrison again?'

'Of course it is. I've got to do something with myself. If I stay at home I shall go mad—or drive you mad with my ranting.'

'But it's unfair of you. Don't you see that?'

'What? Me and William?'

'Yes. You're just using him.'

Maxine shot her sister a look of impatience. 'He's perfectly grown up and I'm sure he's aware of that, but he doesn't seem to mind. He knows something happened between me and Kurt while we were away, he just sensed it, but he doesn't know what. He asked me and I told him I'm not prepared to talk about it. And that was that. He just laughed and said that Kurt Raynor's misfortune is his good fortune. So don't worry for William Harrison.'

'I wasn't,' Polly said quietly. 'I'm worrying about you. I—what shall I tell Kurt if he turns up here this evening?'

'Here? He won't do that. Why should he?'

It was Polly's turn to look impatient. 'Your notice, you idiot. Any minute now, Jim Ferguson will be giving Kurt your letter of resignation. You don't think Kurt isn't going to react to it, do you?'

'Not to the point of turning up on my doorstep, no.' But he would, she felt sure, get on the telephone to her first thing in the morning. At least, she hoped he would. Surely he cared at least that much, enough to make a protest, if only as a matter of simple good manners?

That Kurt was already on his way to her home, Maxine had no way of knowing. Five minutes after her last words to Polly, she was in William's car and they were heading in the direction of Cheltenham. In the dark of the evening, neither of them registered the black Volvo facing them across the road, waiting for the lights to change.

In fact it wasn't until the two cars actually passed that Kurt spotted Maxine—and when he saw who she was with his hands tightened furiously around the steering-wheel. William Harrison! So she was still seeing him. This, after she had explicitly told him it was over.

Maxine arrived home at ten minutes to two and William Harrison went indoors with her. 'Maxine?'

Maxine was too drunk to notice that William was very cross. 'Maxine, are you registering anything I'm saying? What the devil's got into you tonight?'

'The devil.' She answered with a hiccup, dimly aware she was behaving badly but too miserable to care. It had all caught up with her tonight—Kurt's lies, her love for him . . . his lies. Ellen Parker. Ellen Parker and the engagement which might one day turn out to be an engagement again, for all she knew.

She did actually know a few things for definite. She knew she was drunk and she knew that William Harrison bored her out of her skull. She knew she had just crashed into the hall table. She knew Kurt was as devious as devious could be, and she knew she shouldn't love a man like that.

But she did.

There was no doubt about that, not in her mind and not in her heart, either. And if her mind was fuzzy, her heart was not. It didn't lie. Whatever Kurt was or was not, she loved him. It had little to do with the obvious things, how she adored his sense of humour, how she wanted him physically, how she respected him intellectually. It was all of that, certainly, but it was much more besides. She loved him through and through, for everything that he was—or irrespective of what he was . . .

'Maxine!' It wasn't William this time, it was Polly. Alerted by the crash of the hall table and the loud anger of William's voice, she appeared at the top of the stairs flinging her housecoat over her nightie. 'What on earth——'

'Your sister is drunk.' This, from William, or something like that. 'I don't know what got into her tonight, she was pouring wine down like . . .'

Maxine didn't hear the rest of the sentence. People were moving her and suddenly she was sitting on the settee. Then people were moving around and muttering secretively, talking about her. She could hear them, in the kitchen now, using her name and talking about her . . .

CHAPTER NINE

THE alarm sounded like a banshee and the hammering in Maxine's head was excruciating. She made a valiant effort to ignore the latter, reaching out to switch off the alarm clock and knowing she must, simply must, get up.

Polly was already downstairs, as usual. A fresh pot of tea was on the table and she smiled when Maxine sank on to a chair, flinching. 'How are you?'

'What do you think?' She squinted at Polly and waited for the questions. There weren't any. 'Well, big sister, aren't you going to tell me off?'

'For what? For being unhappy? For being in love? Hardly.' There was another smile, infinitely patient. 'But, Max, I am going to give you some advice. Can you take it right now?'

'Depends.' It was very bright in the kitchen. Spring had sprung and the morning sunshine was pouring in, the willow tree in the garden was swaying in the soft breeze outside and Maxine half closed her eyes against the light. 'Try me.'

'I think you should tell Kurt how you feel about him. Tell him you're in love with him.'

It was an amazing cure for a hangover. Maxine stared at Polly as if she had lost her mind. 'Are you off your rocker? Tell him? *Tell* him? And make a complete idiot of myself? No, thank you!'

That was the end of the conversation. Polly opened her mouth to say something further but changed her mind and closed it again. Half an hour later, Maxine was in the shower and feeling a little better for it. But only a little—she wasn't up to coping with the telephone call from an angry William Harrison.

'Maxine? Ah, so you are in the land of the living...'

It took a moment for her to realise who it was. She was upstairs, half dressed, half undressed. 'William?'

'Of course it's me, though I'm quite certain you'd prefer to hear someone else's voice on the line. Last night was a revelation to me, Maxine. I think I've been patient with you...'

She held the receiver away from her ear and looked at it. The man was talking to her as if she were a naughty six-year-old! 'Patient with me? William, listen——'

'No, you listen. Patient, yes, that's what I said. And it got me precisely nowhere with you. I can guess why, and if I needed any further disillusionment I certainly got it last night. You could hardly stand up, you'd never have made it up the drive if I hadn't been there to——'

'I don't need to hear this. I'd appreciate it if——'

'You do need to hear it. I'm not going to ring you again, Maxine, you're a waste of time. You're obviously in love with Raynor—and that's a waste of *your* time! The sooner you see that, the better. Give up on him and get yourself sorted out. When you've achieved that, you can give me a ring.'

She couldn't believe her ears. The arrogance of the man! 'How kind!' she said sweetly. 'But don't hold your breath. Goodbye, William.' She hung up.

Staying right where she was, she stood and looked at the phone for a moment. 'Give up on him.' 'Get yourself sorted out.' Didn't William understand anything? Oh, if only it were that easy!

* * *

There wasn't a word from Kurt. Not a word. No protest at her handing in her notice, nothing at all. It served nicely to show how much he cared. He didn't give a damn whether she stayed on or not. He didn't give a damn, full stop.

It was a relief, his being out of the office for the rest of the week. Maxine saw nothing of him at all. On the Friday morning Jim Ferguson had another go at her about leaving, but there had been no word about it at all from Kurt.

It was Jim's last attempt to dissuade her. 'Maxine, I've been thinking. Kurt's been out of the office all week, and next week he's going to visit the London stores with Linda Storton. In other words he's started to hand over the reins here at Dunn & Dunn. You knew it was going to be predominantly my baby and from now on we won't be seeing much of Kurt. He's virtually told me as much. What I'm trying to say is, this removes your last reason, your real reason, for leaving. So why don't you withdraw your notice?'

'No.'

'Maxine——'

'*No*, Jim. Thanks all the same.'

It had got to the stage where it was hurting just to be on the premises. It was she, now, who looked through the glass partition every time she was on her feet. She was missing Kurt dreadfully.

On Saturday morning the sun was shining and she got up feeling in slightly better spirits. She was going to St Hilda's to collect the children, to take them to the park. Kurt's house, the Manor, stood on the south side of Oldfield's park—but what of it? There was no way she was going to alter her routine just in case she happened to be seen by him.

She was seen by him. Or rather, she saw him first. Had she known for certain that their paths would cross, she would not have been so blasé, she would have taken the children somewhere else. As it was she got to the orphanage in time to help with serving lunch and she had, she was told, been missed.

Mrs MacKinlay, who was in charge of the home, greeted her as though it had been years rather than weeks since she had been there. Mrs MacKinlay had been a friend of Maxine's mother, an infrequent but regular visitor to their house some years ago.

'Maxine! Hello, love. I wasn't sure whether to expect you today, I meant to ring Polly but—oh, you know how busy I am. Well, here you are!'

Maxine smiled. May MacKinlay was chubby and motherly, she talked a lot when she had the chance— and she loved her job. 'Yes, here I am. How's everyone?'

'Tommy Ellison has another cold, he's in bed. Little Marguerite Patel has been asking for you because she wants you to take her to feed the ducks. I mean you, especially,' she added, smiling. 'Richie will be having his sixth birthday next Wednesday and can talk about nothing else. It's—you know, the usual! *But* there is some exciting news. Very exciting.'

'I can't wait.' Maxine laughed. There was rarely exciting news around here. It was a shifting population—children left to live in foster homes, they got adopted, and, while that was exciting for them, for Mrs MacKinlay and her staff it was both a happy and a sad time, a time for goodbyes rather than excitement.

'We have a new minibus. What do you think of that? Brand spanking new—and it was given to us in the strangest manner! We have a new friend but I have no idea who it is. I'm curious,' she added, 'though I shan't lose any sleep over it, I'm just grateful for its delivery!' She let her eyes roll skyward, laughing.

Maxine managed to follow this, just. 'Friends' was the blanket word for people who gave to the charity. All donations were made through head office as a rule—but not on this occasion, apparently.

'And when I say delivery,' Mrs MacKinlay went on, 'I mean just that. You know the Keene garage and car showrooms in Eshford? Well, that's where our old bus came from. 'Course, it was new at the time! Anyway, right out of the blue, last Saturday morning, a new bus was delivered by one of their salesmen. He said it was a donation from someone who wished to remain anonymous. What do you think of that? And there it was, complete with log-book and road tax paid for a full year—and it was already painted with our name on it, just exactly like the old bus, in the same colours and all. What,' she said again, 'do you think of that?'

This time Maxine got a chance to say what she thought of it. 'I think that's wonderful. How kind of—someone!'

She took six children out that day, in the new bus, six of the youngest ones. The older children had better things to do—they weren't interested in feeding ducks or going on the playground in the park.

Marguerite and Richie almost came to blows; she wanted to head for the pond, he wanted to head for the playground. Maxine sat on a park bench, gathered all six children around her and took a vote on it. 'Which do we do first? Those who want to go to the pond first, hands up.' It was fifty-fifty. 'Right, then I have the casting vote.'

'What does that mean?' one of them wanted to know.

'It means I have a say in the matter. We go to the playground first.' There was a good reason for this—the fact that the playground was nearer than the pond.

By the time the children had tired themselves on swings and slides and climbing-frames, it was three o'clock; they did not tire easily. At least they were in gentler spirits by the time they were communing with the ducks, and it was then that Maxine saw Kurt. She had to look twice because he was at a distance—but her heart knew who it was before her eyes could be certain, and it started pounding like a mad thing, making her breathless and panicky. He was dressed in a navy tracksuit, a sweat band around his head, and was jogging along the path with two dogs at his heels, two young, gorgeous golden Labradors.

She turned away immediately, her attention fully on the ducks, hoping he hadn't spotted her.

He had spotted her. In less than a minute he was by her side, panting slightly and unsmiling. He said something but she didn't hear him for the cacophony that was the children squealing delightedly over the dogs. There was an immediate and prolonged fuss, children over dogs and dogs over children. Maxine looked anxiously at Kurt—to see him laughing. He had stooped to restrain Richie from pulling at a dog's tail. 'No, no, son, she won't take kindly to that! How would you like it if someone pulled your tail?'

'I haven't got a tail, mister!'

'You haven't, eh? Well then, how would you like it if she nipped you on the seat of your pants?'

Richie didn't seem to like the sound of that. 'Is he vicious?'

'She,' Kurt amended. 'They're both bitches. And no, they're not vicious, far from it. They're friendly but they don't like having their tails pulled.'

'What are they called?'

'How old are they?'

'What kind of dogs are they?'

The questions came thick and fast. Kurt answered them all laughingly, much to Maxine's astonishment, still with his knees bent so he was nearer their height. She had been forgotten; she watched the scene feeling convinced that her heart would stop beating altogether if it didn't stop beating so fast.

It felt like an age since she had seen him. 'Kurt...'

The word came quietly but he heard it. He stood up, looking down at her now, but she didn't really know what to say, there was so *much* she wanted to say. She wanted to accuse him, to fling Ellen Parker up at him. She wanted to thrash out; she also wanted to cry and was fighting it with everything in her. And she wanted *him* to say something, for him at least to mention her handing her notice in. Why, why hadn't he said anything? If for no other reason than that she was a good secretary, why hadn't he phoned her and protested?

But he made no mention of it. He did smile, at last, but it was far from being a warm smile and he made no mention at all of work. 'How are you, Maxine? You seem to be coping well enough.' He gestured towards the children.

'I—yes. I—didn't know you had dogs.'

He looked straight at her. 'For company,' he said.

'But didn't you tell me you have a couple living with you? A housekeeper and gardener-cum-handyman?'

'They're staff and they're married and they live their lives quite separately from me. They have a flat in the east wing of the house.'

Maxine glanced across the park. From where they stood she could see the imposing outline of the Manor.

'Would you——?' Kurt changed his mind; he turned instead to the children. 'Listen, you guys, my new house is very much in need of a house-warming, so how would you like to come home with me and have tea and cakes?'

There was another babble of excitement. One of the children wanted to know if there would be real cream in the cakes, two others said yes without question, another said, 'But we don't even know you,' and Marguerite asked if they could finish feeding the ducks first.

It was, surprisingly, Richie who turned to Maxine, his young face a picture of eagerness. 'Will it be OK? Oh, do say yes!'

Kurt was watching her. 'Well, O mistress? Why don't you make some introductions, then you can say yes and it will all be safe and respectable?' He glanced at the children, his eyes challenging when they came back to hers. He had put her on the spot; the youngsters were carrying on so, it was impossible to say no. She made the introductions and it was while she was doing so that the realisation dawned on her, and when it did it came as a shock, so much so that she almost forgot what she was doing. She had been wrong, absolutely wrong in assuming that Kurt disliked children. There was no way that someone who had no interest in children would invite a horde of them home for tea, just like that!

'Where's this decrepit minibus of yours?' Kurt wanted to know. 'Which side of the park?'

'It's parked near the gates on the west. I'll fetch it later, we can walk to your house.'

'What does decrepit mean?' The question came from Marguerite; she turned away from the ducks to ask it.

'It means old and battered, rather like me.' Kurt scooped her up in his arms, much to her delight. 'Come on, any more of that and the ducks will have indigestion!'

The gang of them started walking, with the dogs yapping and the children telling Kurt, protesting to Kurt, that their minibus was *not* old and battered, it was a new one and it was very smart, in fact it was the nicest in the whole country.

'I see. Then pardon me, my friends.'

'If you like,' Richie volunteered, 'you can see it for yourself later!'

Kurt turned, then, to glance at Maxine. She had been hanging back a little, a myriad emotions churning inside her as she watched him, love battling against resentment, anger battling against tenderness. Marguerite was still in his arms, he seemed perfectly content to have her there and the sight touched Maxine deeply, as did his manner. He was marvellous with children. Why had she assumed he didn't care for them?

Just as Kurt had been when she had first met him, the Manor was also quite unlike what she had expected. It was not the showpiece one might presume it to be from its smart exterior, it was a home, spacious and cosy at the same time, comfortable without being fussy. Nor was it predominantly masculine, as she had imagined; there were flowers in every room, colourful paintings on the walls, a few ornaments here and there. From the hall they cut through the dining-room to the drawing-room, where Maxine sat with the children while Kurt summoned his housekeeper.

'Mrs Harvey, say hello to some of my new friends from St Hilda's—and Miss Maxine Smith. Maxine, this is Mrs Harvey whose cooking is so good it's almost sinful. As for her baking, her *cakes*,' he added, with a smile at the children, 'well, why don't you wait and see?'

Maxine shook hands with the housekeeper, an apologetic look on her face, feeling as sorry for the woman as she did for herself. Oh, Kurt was being civilised enough towards her, but underlying that there was coldness and it was hurting. It was hurting like hell in spite of her anger towards him. 'This wasn't my idea, Mrs Harvey, I promise you. Can you cope with tea for eight?'

'No problem at all! My dear, I brought up five children of my own. Mind you, they're all grown up and off my hands now, thank heavens—not that I'd have been without them, any of 'em. Mr Raynor, would you like me to see to the little ones in the kitchen?'

'Certainly not, they're my guests and they'll all have tea in here.'

'As you wish.' Mrs Harvey retreated with a grin, saying something about having a batch of scones in the oven.

Maxine looked around, feeling the need to say something. Through the big picture windows overlooking the back of the house she could see a tennis-court. 'It—it's a lovely house, Kurt. Must be nice to have your own tennis-court.'

'Yes. Of course the place is too big for just one. But who knows? I still have hopes of marrying and having a family of my own.'

A family of his own. Why hadn't she thought of that when she had jumped to the wrong conclusion? Kurt had never known his father, he had no brothers or sisters, he had had only his mother. It made sense that he would want a family around him.

'There's a swimming-pool, Kurt's got a swimming-pool! And it's *inside*!' The voice came from the doorway and it belonged to Richie. Maxine scolded him; she hadn't even noticed he'd left the room.

'Richie! You do not go wandering around people's houses unless you have been invited to. Now come here and sit down!'

But the damage was already done. The children were ooh-ing and aah-ing at the idea of someone having their very own swimming-pool and Kurt had little choice but to invite them to take a look—not that he seemed to mind. They all trooped after him down the hall, in the direction opposite the front door, Maxine included.

It was gorgeous, a huge, cleverly designed room with a twinkling blue pool, the biggest she had ever seen in a house. There was a sitting area near the windows overlooking the garden, a bar and lots of pot plants for greenery and softness. Maxine looked longingly at the water, knowing it would be warm. Needless to say, the children were having similiar thoughts.

'No.' She spoke very firmly, looking warningly at Kurt. They were asking him if they could swim—and he had not refused them anything so far.

'No.' He echoed Maxine, ignoring her warning look. 'Because you have no costumes with you, and in any case you would have to have permission from—whoever is in charge.'

'Maxine is——'

'Mrs MacKinlay is in charge.' Maxine wagged her finger at all six. '*Her* permission would be needed, not mine.'

'And what if she says yes?'

'You could telephone her and ask.' This, from Richie. 'I don't mind going in bare!'

'I do! I mean I'm not!' Marguerite's expression was one of such horror that Maxine couldn't help laughing.

'Kurt—look what you've done! I hope you're proud of yourself.'

'Proud of myself?' He came over to her, lowering his voice as he went on, with undisguised anger on his face. 'What about you, Maxine? Are you proud of yourself, proud of your cowardice, your stubbornness, your blindness?'

So he was finally getting around to the matter of her resignation! But his tone, low and bitter, stunned her for a moment, a moment during which all the anger and resentment she felt came flooding to the surface. Had the housekeeper not stuck her head around the door to say that tea was served in the drawing-room, Maxine would have exploded. As it was, the children all disappeared in a flash and she, too, turned to go.

'Hold it! I asked you a question, Maxine.' The grip on her shoulder was painful—and that was more than enough for her.

She rounded on Kurt furiously, pushing his hand away with a look of utter distaste. 'Don't touch me! I can't stand it. I can't stand *you*. My cowardice, you call it? My stubbornness? What about your deception, your——'

'I told you before, the night of your birthday was not a set-up.'

'I'm not referring to that.' It was all she could do not to yell at him, to strike out physically. Had there been no danger of being overheard by the children, she might have done both. 'I'm referring to Ellen Parker and your so-called platonic relationship with her. You were out with her last Saturday, I am informed—just two days after doing your utmost to get me into bed!' Her voice was rising in spite of herself, her eyes flashing the fury she felt. 'What kind of behaviour do you call that? Well, if you think me a coward, Kurt Raynor, I'm telling you you're a louse, a rotten, two-timing *louse*.'

'You've got it all wrong——' That was as far as he got.

Richie appeared in the doorway, looking afraid. 'Maxine? Why are you two shouting at each other?'

'Go and have your tea, Richie.' It took all her self-control not to shout at the child, too. 'Go on, poppet, I'll be with you in a minute.'

'You're coming as well, aren't you, Kurt?'

'Of course.' It came quietly, calmly, and was accompanied by a smile.

The moment Richie retreated, Kurt continued in the same quiet voice . . . but it was dangerously quiet now. His eyes locked on to Maxine's with a silent warning. 'Now you listen and listen well. There is nothing between me and Ellen Parker, there hasn't been for years. She came to see me last Saturday to——'

'Save it, Kurt! Don't insult me with more lies.'

'Dammit, woman, I said listen to me!' Both hands were on her shoulders suddenly and she was being shaken so hard she thought her head would fall off. Frantically she pushed against his chest with both hands, putting enough distance between them so she could strike out. Her right hand was caught in midair, inches from his face. 'Don't try it, Maxine! Do that again and you'll get more than you're bargaining for—you'll find yourself over my knee getting the spanking you richly deserve. You just don't know what you're talking about as far as Ellen's concerned. You've got it all wrong, completely wrong. Well, you can think what you like. I'm past caring. There's just no getting through to you—but I'll tell you this: don't think for one second that I'm entirely taken in by you. I'm aware of your little ego trip with the good doctor Harrison. *You* were out with *him* last Monday—I am informed.' The last three words were added facetiously. 'And you're about to tell me now that your relationship with him is platonic, aren't you?'

'Of course I am.' The words were out before she could think. He was informed? By whom? Who had seen her out with William?

'And why should I believe that? Eh? Why, when you told me several weeks ago that you'd finished with him?'

'I had. I——' She stopped abruptly, recognising the danger she was in. If she explained about William she would paint herself neatly into a corner. There was simply nothing she could add. To let Kurt know she had gone out with William on the rebound would be tantamount to letting Kurt know how important he was to her.

'Exactly!' There was triumph in his voice. 'You're the one who lied—and it's your ongoing affair with Harrison that made you hold out on me when we were away together.' Carefully, Kurt watched her face, her eyes, waiting and hoping for a reaction. There was none forthcoming and inwardly he marvelled at the extent of her stubbornness. Or was it pride? What was it that prevented her from defending herself? Not for one moment did he think she was going to bed with Harrison—he doubted she had been to bed with anyone, her ex-fiancé included. But she was not reacting—she was walking away! She seemed content to let him believe what he was appearing to believe. 'Maxine?'

'Go to hell, Kurt! The same applies. You can think what you like about me, I just don't care.' Blindly she groped for the door-handle, knowing that if she stayed alone with him for a second longer she would break down and make a complete fool of herself. She had to get to the children and, somehow, she had to get through this teatime charade with her dignity intact.

The following hour was agonising. She felt that Kurt had issued this invitation to punish her somehow, although it was obvious how much he enjoyed children—and they him. In other circumstances his way with them would have been a delight to watch. He controlled them with a firm but gentle manner, never needing to resort to a raised voice. It was an ability she envied; she often had to shout to get through to them.

Surreptitiously she kept checking her watch, telling herself that they would leave as soon as it was reasonable to do so. At four-thirty she got to her feet. 'Right, gang, we have to go now.' She held up a hand at their protests. 'You know as well as I do that we have to be back at St Hilda's by five o'clock—and no later! Now come along.'

Kurt got lazily to his feet, reminding her that he had been promised a look at their new bus. 'I'll walk over to the car park with you.'

Every step was an agony to Maxine. *Was* he doing this on purpose, all of it? But why should he, what sense would that make?

It was another five minutes before she could get away from him, and by then he had admired the bus with such enthusiasm she ought to have been able to laugh. She couldn't; she climbed into the driver's seat while Kurt saw the children settled in the back, then he got out and paused by her window. 'You can bring the children any time, Maxine, for a swim on Saturdays. If permission is given. Just give me a little notice.'

She could do no more than stare at him in disbelief. This, when in two weeks' time she would be leaving his employ? When they clearly had nothing more to say to one another now—now or ever? 'I—that's very kind of you but I think you'd regret it. There are about twenty-five children at St Hilda's at any given time and they'd all want to come. The older ones might not care for playgrounds but they'd jump at the idea of swimming in a private indoor pool.'

'So? Bring them half a dozen at a time, let them have turns each.'

'No. Thanks all the same. You'd be biting off more than you could chew.'

'You mean you don't think you and I could supervise them?'

'No, I mean——'

'I know what you mean.' He interrupted her impatiently. His irritation was barely suppressed and she felt as if her heart were being crushed. 'You mean you don't want to be the one to bring them. I should have realised, but there are times when I'm still fool enough to hope you'll change.'

Again she stared at him. 'Change? What kind of change?'

'Think about it,' he said as he walked away. 'Just think about it.'

CHAPTER TEN

MAXINE couldn't stop thinking about it; she couldn't get Kurt out of her mind for one minute. When she got home that evening, it was to face an empty house. Polly was at David's for the weekend, which meant she wouldn't see her until Monday evening. She made herself a snack and watched TV for an hour, not that she registered much.

She almost jumped out of her skin when the telephone rang.

'Max? How are you doing?' It was Polly, concerned for her, checking on her.

'I'm OK.'

'Really? Are you really all right? Do you want to talk? I'll come home tonight if——'

'No. I'm going to bed early, the children have worn me out today.' Maxine was desperate to talk but she wasn't going to spoil her sister's weekend, or David's. 'But I'm fine, Polly, just tired. I'll see you after work on Monday.'

'OK—but I'll be late, we've got a staff meeting and it might go on for some time.'

Monday seemed a long way away—there was Sunday to get through first, and that was a day which dragged. There was no relaxation for Maxine even though she lay around idly, attempting to read the newspapers but unable to concentrate on anything.

She was the same in the office the following morning; she got there on time but she couldn't apply her mind to anything and she was staring into space when Jim Ferguson came in. When he opened the door to her office, she spun round on her typing chair so fast that she almost crashed into his legs as he approached her desk. 'Jim!'

He smiled, but there was a worried look in his eyes. 'Hey, I work here, remember?'

'I'm sorry, I'm ... not myself today.'

'You and Kurt Raynor.'

'What do you mean? Have you spoken to him? Is he coming in?'

The boss sat down and shook his head at her. 'No, he is not coming in. I've just been on the phone to him and he's in one hell of a bad mood. Linda Storton tells me he's been like that for days. Now, it wouldn't have anything to do with you, would it?'

Maxine eyed him suspiciously. 'Why? What has he been saying to you?'

'Not a thing, but then he wouldn't.' He leaned forward, his eyes meeting hers directly. 'I mean, if he should happen to have something highly personal on his mind, for example, he wouldn't tell anyone, not even me. I think that's something to do with his upbringing, always trying to be an emotional tough guy.'

'An emotional tough guy? You mean because of his missing father?'

'That, and his mother's suicide. Oh, hell!' Jim saw the expression on her face; it said it all. 'You didn't know about *that* did you? Didn't you know Kurt was brought up in an orphanage?'

'No,' she whispered. 'No, I had no idea.'

Jim looked heavenward. 'He's going to be hopping mad with me if he discovers I've told you this.'

'Don't worry about that, I shan't say anything.' She looked down at her hands, knowing that Kurt would have told her himself, in time...if there had been more time. 'He had told me a lot, he—just omitted the nasty bits, or should I say the very nasty bits.'

'There are very few people who know about his roots, very few, because he scoffs at the story. He calls it his sob story.'

Maxine nodded, remembering how Kurt had seemed reluctant to talk about his childhood. No wonder he hadn't told her the whole of it—it was the kind of classic story one read about and shuddered at, and he would have hated it if she had sympathised. 'But—why an orphanage? Weren't there any other relatives at that time?'

'I don't know. His mother got into trouble when she was seventeen, apparently, and shortly after Kurt was born she committed suicide. I think we can assume she had parents but—obviously they didn't want to know the baby any more than its father did.'

There was a silence followed by, 'Maxine? Is there anything you want to tell me?'

'No.' Then, with sudden realisation, she said, 'The minibus at St Hilda's! It was Kurt who paid for that, wasn't it?'

Jim frowned. 'Of course. Kurt is always giving to children's charities. How come you didn't know about the bus? It was you who told him the old one was falling to pieces. He got on to me first thing on the Monday morning and told me to organise a new one. He told me to keep it strictly anonymous but I took it for granted you would know.'

Maxine shook her head, it was all she could do; she didn't dare attempt speech because she knew she would burst into tears if she did.

'Look,' Jim said quietly, 'neither you nor Kurt have been your normal selves since you came back from the sales trip. Now, I don't believe that you and he fought while you were away, I think you fell in love.'

In the ensuing silence, Maxine kept her eyes fixed firmly on her typewriter. 'This is none of your business,' she managed equally quietly.

'Well, I'm making it my business.' The gently accented voice held no ring of apology. 'Because there are times when Kurt Raynor can be just as guarded as you are, particularly over emotional matters, as I said. So what are you going to do, Maxine?'

'I—don't know what you mean. There's nothing *to* do. You're quite wrong, anyway. Kurt didn't fall in love with me——' She broke off just in time, only to have Jim finish the sentence for her.

'But you did fall in love with him.'

'Jim——'

'No, I haven't finished. If you're going to make any progress at all now, you'll have to tell Kurt how you feel. It'll have to come from you because he's too insecure to be the one to open up first.'

'Insecure? Kurt Raynor, insecure?'

'Haven't you been listening to me? Emotionally, Maxine, emotionally. Think about it.'

Think about it. Those were the last words Kurt had said to her, too. Nevertheless, she shook her head, not wanting Jim to know the strength of her feelings. 'It's academic anyway, as far as I'm concerned. It's my belief that Kurt's still carrying a torch for his ex-fiancée.'

There was unexpected laughter at that. 'Ellen? No way! Oh, he still sees her now and then, but that's for her sake. In reality she's something of a pain sometimes.' He laughed again when he saw Maxine's head snap up in shock. 'He's *told* me as much, I promise you.'

'But——'

'But nothing.' He shrugged, speaking deliberately casually. 'So if perchance you're thinking there's still something going on between them...in some way...forget it.'

The phone rang at that instant and, when Maxine seemed not to notice, Jim picked it up. After that, it was business as usual and he said no more about the big boss.

Polly got home around nine that night, apologising for her lateness and fuming about the staff meeting and the disagreements which had abounded. 'And the worse of it is I had an argument with David, too.'

'During the meeting, you mean?'

'During and afterwards—in the car park. It's nothing personal, it was about school matters, but still! I drove away in one direction and he in another and we were both in a huff.'

They ate the casserole Maxine had waiting in the oven and then settled in the living-room with a tray of coffee.

'So what about you, Max? How was your day? More to the point, how are you, really?'

'I'm——' That was as far as she got. All the tension of the past ten days, all the pent-up tears finally came together and, without warning, the floodgates opened and she cried her eyes out. Then, at last, she was able to talk sensibly. She told Polly of her exchange with Kurt in his house the previous Saturday and of the conversation she'd had with Jim Ferguson that day.

'Max, Max, you're such an idiot...' Polly held her tightly, almost crooning the reprimand. 'When are you going to start trusting yourself? When are you going to trust other people again?'

The questions hit Maxine with such force that Polly might just as well have slapped her. '*What?* Why did you say that?' Her head jerked up, the last of her tears abating. She hadn't told Polly all the things Kurt had said to her, how he had said exactly the same thing. 'What do you mean?' she demanded.

'I mean you're not giving Kurt a chance. For all he knows, you *are* still in love with Francis Lyon. He saw you behaving like a nervous wreck when you bumped into him, so he might think you still care for him.'

'No, I made it clear that I felt nothing for Francis.'

'All right,' Polly sighed, 'then, for all Kurt knows, you are having an affair with William Harrison.'

'No, Polly. He can't really believe that, not after the way we——'

'What? The way you didn't go to bed together?' There was a pause, a wry smile, a little time for the point to penetrate—a pause during which the doorbell rang.

Polly got to her feet to answer it. 'Bother! Now who can that be? What a time for someone to call.

Maxine panicked. 'Don't let them in, whoever it is. I mean, let me get out of the way first.' She had no intention of anyone seeing her in this state. She followed her sister into the hall and dashed up the stairs; her bedroom door was not quite shut before she heard Polly's, 'David!'

She groaned inwardly, which was selfish, she knew, because the pleasure in her sister's voice had been unmistakable. Her feud with her fiancé was about to be resolved—and he was the one extending the olive-branch. Well, good for them.

Resignedly she washed her face and brushed her teeth; she might as well go to bed now. She was doing just that when Polly came in.

'Maxine? I'm sorry. I'll tell him to go—when we've sorted out our differences.'

'No, it's all right, really it is. I have some thinking to do and I'd just as soon be alone.'

'But——'

'No, honestly, Polly, I really do want to be alone.'

'Well, if you're sure...' Her sister retreated dubiously, casting an anxious look over her shoulder as she closed the door.

Maxine switched off the lamp and lay flat on her back, her eyes wide open. One question was rolling round and round in her mind, not Polly's words but Kurt's. Last Saturday he had asked her whether she was proud of her cowardice, her stubbornness, her blindness. He had also said he was fool enough to hope she would change.

And he had *not* been talking about her resignation from the company.

Was Jim Ferguson right? Was there a chance that Kurt loved her? He had never given her a hint of it . . . but then neither had she of her love for him. She had very carefully kept her feelings hidden from him.

She sat bolt upright and snapped on the lamp. She had to tell Kurt how she really felt; she had to talk to him. It was up to her and it was she who had to go to him—because she had been just as much the emotional tough guy as he had. It was imperative she talk to him—right now!

A glance at her bedside clock told her it was ten minutes to midnight. But what of it? If David could drive all the way from Oxford to talk to Polly at this hour, Maxine could go to Kurt.

She flung back the bedclothes—and then she stopped, sitting utterly still. She was scared suddenly, not knowing whether Kurt would welcome her pouring her heart out, not knowing how he would react. What if Jim Ferguson had it all wrong? She flopped back on the bed. How *would* he react? Oh, if only she had the answer to that!

She switched off the lamp and lay down again—only to flick the light back on seconds later, realising that it was her own instincts she must act upon, not the opinions of others. Whether Jim was right or whether he was wrong didn't matter—she was going to trust *herself*.

Suddenly she was smiling, smiling and knowing, and in permitting this knowingness full rein she realised that Kurt already knew she was in love with him—so why was she wasting time?

She was flinging on jeans and a sweater when Polly tapped at her door. 'Max? Are you all right? What are you doing?'

Maxine was laughing. 'I'm going to Kurt, that's what I'm doing!'

Polly's face broke into a smile. 'About time, too! Good luck—and don't drive too fast.'

Maxine did drive too fast—she was round at the Manor in no time, wondering whether Kurt would be in bed. Apart from an outside lamp there was no light showing at the front of the house. She drove around to the back and came to a crunching halt on the gravel, seeing that the living-room lights were on.

Kurt was at the kitchen door before she had even got out of the car, looking puzzled and positively displeased—until he registered who his late-night visitor was.

'Maxine?'

She walked towards him with a confidence that was genuine, her smile reflecting warmly in her eyes. 'I've decided I should give you the opportunity to explain about Ellen Parker, after all,' she said softly.

'Oh, you have, have you?'

For one heart-stopping moment, Maxine thought she had let things go too far, that she and the stubbornness she'd been born with had left things too late. It was not until the light from the kitchen caught Kurt's eyes that she saw the laughter dancing in their brown depths. And then she knew there had been no risk at all. Coming here had not been a mistake... it was the sanest thing she had done in her entire life.

'I'm delighted to hear it.' Kurt's arms came around her. They were standing on the kitchen step and were getting rained on. 'But that isn't why you came, Maxine. At least, it's only part of why you came. Now,' he commanded, 'tell me what you really came to say.'

In the face of her deliberate, teasing silence, he almost exploded. 'Don't just stand there smiling at me, say it!'

She was safe, so was he. They both knew it and there was no longer any hurry. 'I'll tell you this,' she began, smiling wickedly, 'we're both getting drenched.'

'Never mind *that*! Say what you came to say, woman!'

'Do you think I could come in first?'

He whisked her clean off the floor, scooping her up in his arms as easily as he had scooped up little Marguerite. Unceremoniously he dumped her in the kitchen and shook her. 'Maxine Smith, if you keep me waiting one moment longer, I shan't be responsible for my actions! Now tell me you love me at once!'

'I love you,' she said. 'I love you, I love you, I love—— '

That was enough for Kurt; he brought his mouth down to hers to kiss her slowly and with exquisite tenderness. When he raised his head she could see that same tenderness reflected in his eyes. 'What are we doing, standing here? Come, my darling, come sit by the fire with me, you're shivering.'

She wasn't shivering, she was trembling, trembling at the touch of his arm around her waist, trembling because all the uncertainty was over. 'I'm not cold, I'm just happy.'

'Sit,' he said, pushing her gently on to the settee nearest the fire just the same. 'Now come closer, I want you in my arms and I want you to listen to me. Ellen Parker and I——'

'It doesn't matter.' Maxine shook her head, no longer doubting what he had told her before. Perhaps she never had, in her heart of hearts, because whatever Kurt was he was not a liar.

'It does matter, Maxine. I want to tell you, I don't want even a shadow of a doubt in your mind. Ellen and I were lovers once, obviously, but that was a long time ago. It's very simple, really—she and I see each other occasionally and it's usually when she needs someone to tell her troubles to. A neutral ear, if you see what I mean. She's been living and working in London this past ten years. Anyhow, she phoned me and invited herself to see my new house. It's very different from the home I had in London, so I made a date with her and took her to dinner after showing her around the Manor. That was when you saw us in the Copper Kettle.'

He looked at her closely. 'You do believe me? The relationship is platonic.'

'I believe you. But—what happened between you two?'

'I was in love with her, eight years ago, and there was nothing false about it. The trouble was that it didn't last and that was because I didn't know her, I mean really know her. You see, incredible though it seems, it wasn't until we were actually engaged that we got around to discussing children.'

'Children? Well, that's certainly a major consideration!'

'Quite. Yet somehow we'd each assumed that we held the same views about having a family. But we didn't, they couldn't have been more opposed—very strongly opposed. Like me, Ellen's always known her own mind and she still does. She absolutely didn't want to have children.'

'I—did she never marry, then?'

'She did, yes.' Kurt shook his head. 'And that was a very sad business. She tells me that she and her husband were very compatible, ideal for each other she said, but—she was widowed after five months. He was killed in a car crash. It was soon after that that she contacted me again and I started seeing her now and then. She needed someone to talk to.'

'And now?'

'She's happy enough these days. She's about to emigrate to America and that's why she was here last week—to say goodbye.'

Silence reigned until Maxine broke it. 'So, since Ellen there's—I mean, you've never committed yourself to anyone since then?'

'No. Because I've never met anyone I want to commit myself to—but that's the only reason,' he added pointedly. 'It's not because I'm afraid of commitment.'

Maxine smiled inwardly. Of course he was afraid of commitment, despite his having entered into it once.

This was why he had recognised so rapidly the fear she had known about it. He, too, had made a mistake, and, although he had adjusted to a broken engagement better than she had, he still bore emotional scars whereas she no longer did. His were from a different source; they were not from his engagement but from the distant past, his upbringing. What rejection he must have felt in his formative years—a father who didn't want to know him and a mother who committed suicide!

'Maxine . . .'

She looked into his eyes and knew what he was going to say. His heart was in his eyes, the tenderness of his expression making her want to weep. She could hardly bear it, because there was uncertainty there, too. But she couldn't help him over the moment. All she could do was nod, speechlessly, when he asked her to marry him.

'You know,' he murmured, gathering her into his arms again, 'I loved you the moment I set eyes on you. I told myself it was impossible at the time, but there it was.'

'Impossible? You thought that? I find that reassuring, Kurt. I mean, it ought to be impossible. How can one love a total stranger?'

He smiled. 'Don't waste your time puzzling over it, it just happened. It just is. Oh, Maxine, I've had to be so cautious with you. In the beginning I was afraid I'd frighten you off before you even got to know me, before you gave me a chance, yourself a chance, *us* a chance.'

'I know. I'm sorry.' He told her not to be, but she was thinking about the person she had been and the person she now was, one who was able to trust herself and her own instincts again. 'Looking back,' she said,

'I think I loved you on sight, too. At least, I think at some level I knew it, but of course there was no way I would acknowledge it.'

'You did know it,' Kurt said softly, moving his hand so it was nestling between her breasts, a little to the left. 'You knew it in here, where it counts.'

Unable to resist the tease, she smiled another wicked smile, moving his hand so it was covering her breast. 'You won't mind if I invite one of my ex-lovers to our wedding, will you?'

'Not in the least,' came the quick reply, delivered very drily. 'And who might that be? It wouldn't be the good doctor, by any chance?'

'Well, according to you, yes.'

'And according to you?'

She tried to look mysterious. All it provoked, however, was laughter. 'You and William Harrison? Come off it, Maxine!'

This time she tried to look indignant. 'What's that supposed to mean? What's wrong with him?'

'It would be more to the point to ask me what's wrong with you.'

'All right, what's wrong with me?'

'Oh, not a lot.' His laughter was low and deep as he gathered her closer. 'Just a little lack of experience,' he added, bringing his mouth down to hers. 'Nothing that can't very easily be remedied...'

HARLEQUIN

Romance

A Christmas tradition...

Imagine spending Christmas in New
Orleans with a blind stranger and his aged
guide dog—when you're supposed to be
there on your honeymoon!
#3163 Every Kind of Heaven
by Bethany Campbell

Imagine spending Christmas with a man
you once "married"—in a mock ceremony
at the age of eight!
#3166 The Forgetful Bride
by Debbie Macomber

*Available in December 1991, wherever
Harlequin books are sold.*

RXM

HISTORICAL

CHRISTMAS

STORIES · 1991

Bring back heartwarming memories of Christmas past
with HISTORICAL CHRISTMAS STORIES 1991,
a collection of romantic stories
by three popular authors.
The perfect Christmas gift!

Don't miss these heartwarming stories,
available in November
wherever Harlequin books are sold:

CHRISTMAS YET TO COME
by Linda Trent
A SEASON OF JOY
by Caryn Cameron
FORTUNE'S GIFT
by DeLoras Scott

**Best Wishes and Season's Greetings
from Harlequin!**

XM-91

HARLEQUIN

Romance

This December, travel to Northport, Massachusetts, with Harlequin Romance FIRST CLASS title #3164, A TOUCH OF FORGIVENESS by Emma Goldrick

Folks in Northport called Kitty the meanest woman in town, but she couldn't forget how they had duped her brother and exploited her family's land. It was hard to be mean, though, when Joel Carmody was around—his calm, good humor made Kitty feel like a new woman. Nevertheless, a Carmody was a Carmody, and the name meant money and power to the townspeople.... Could Kitty really trust Joel, or was he like all the rest?

Reach for the stars with

Harlequin Superromance®

in a new trilogy by award-winning author Pamela Bauer

Family ties...

Seventh Heaven (title #481)
Kate Osborne feels she needs to watch out for her daughters. But it seems she isn't the only one watching! Police Commissioner Donovan Cade appears to have a telescope trained on her oldest daughter's bedroom window! Protest leads to passion as Kate discovers Donovan's true interests.
Coming in December

On Cloud Nine (title #484)
Kate's second daughter, Juliet, has old-fashioned values like her mother's. But those values are tested when she meets Ross Stafford, a jazz musician and teaching assistant . . . and the object of her younger sister's affections. Can Juliet only achieve her heart's desire at the cost of her integrity?
Coming in January

Swinging On a Star (title #487)
Meridee is Kate's oldest daughter, but very much her own person. Determined to climb the corporate ladder, she has never had time for love. But her life is turned upside down when Zeb Farrell storms into town, determined to eliminate jobs in her company— her sister's among them! Meridee is prepared to do battle, but for once, she's met her match.
Coming in February

"INDULGE A LITTLE" SWEEPSTAKES

HERE'S HOW THE SWEEPSTAKES WORKS

NO PURCHASE NECESSARY

To enter each drawing, complete the appropriate Official Entry Form or a 3" by 5" index card by hand-printing your name, address and phone number and the trip destination that the entry is being submitted for (i.e., Walt Disney World Vacation Drawing, etc.) and mailing it to: Indulge '91 Subscribers-Only Sweepstakes, P.O. Box 1397, Buffalo, New York 14269-1397.

No responsibility is assumed for lost, late or misdirected mail. Entries must be sent separately with first class postage affixed, and be received by: 9/30/91 for the Walt Disney World Vacation Drawing, 10/31/91 for the Alaskan Cruise Drawing and 11/30/91 for the Hawaiian Vacation Drawing. Sweepstakes is open to residents of the U.S. and Canada, 21 years of age or older as of 11/7/91.

For complete rules, send a self-addressed, stamped (WA residents need not affix return postage) envelope to: Indulge '91 Subscribers-Only Sweepstakes Rules, P.O. Box 4005, Blair, NE 68009.

© 1991 HARLEQUIN ENTERPRISES LTD.   DIR-RL

"INDULGE A LITTLE" SWEEPSTAKES

HERE'S HOW THE SWEEPSTAKES WORKS

NO PURCHASE NECESSARY

To enter each drawing, complete the appropriate Official Entry Form or a 3" by 5" index card by hand-printing your name, address and phone number and the trip destination that the entry is being submitted for (i.e., Walt Disney World Vacation Drawing, etc.) and mailing it to: Indulge '91 Subscribers-Only Sweepstakes, P.O. Box 1397, Buffalo, New York 14269-1397.

No responsibility is assumed for lost, late or misdirected mail. Entries must be sent separately with first class postage affixed, and be received by: 9/30/91 for the Walt Disney World Vacation Drawing, 10/31/91 for the Alaskan Cruise Drawing and 11/30/91 for the Hawaiian Vacation Drawing. Sweepstakes is open to residents of the U.S. and Canada, 21 years of age or older as of 11/7/91.

For complete rules, send a self-addressed, stamped (WA residents need not affix return postage) envelope to: Indulge '91 Subscribers-Only Sweepstakes Rules, P.O. Box 4005, Blair, NE 68009.

© 1991 HARLEQUIN ENTERPRISES LTD.   DIR-RL

INDULGE A LITTLE—WIN A LOT!

Summer of '91 Subscribers-Only Sweepstakes

OFFICIAL ENTRY FORM

This entry must be received by: Oct. 31, 1991
This month's winner will be notified by: Nov. 7, 1991
Trip must be taken between: May 27, 1992—Sept. 9, 1992
(depending on sailing schedule)

YES, I want to win the Alaska Cruise vacation for two. I understand the prize includes round-trip airfare, one-week cruise including private cabin, all meals and pocket money as revealed on the "wallet" scratch-off card.

Name _____

Address_____ Apt. _____

City _____

State/Prov. _____ Zip/Postal Code _____

Daytime phone number _____
(Area Code)

Return entries with invoice in envelope provided. Each book in this shipment has two entry coupons—and the more coupons you enter, the better your chances of winning!

© 1991 HARLEQUIN ENTERPRISES LTD.   2N-CPS

INDULGE A LITTLE—WIN A LOT!

Summer of '91 Subscribers-Only Sweepstakes

OFFICIAL ENTRY FORM

This entry must be received by: Oct. 31, 1991
This month's winner will be notified by: Nov. 7, 1991
Trip must be taken between: May 27, 1992—Sept. 9, 1992
(depending on sailing schedule)

YES, I want to win the Alaska Cruise vacation for two. I understand the prize includes round-trip airfare, one-week cruise including private cabin, all meals and pocket money as revealed on the "wallet" scratch-off card.

Name _____

Address_____ Apt. _____

City _____

State/Prov. _____ Zip/Postal Code _____

Daytime phone number _____
(Area Code)

Return entries with invoice in envelope provided. Each book in this shipment has two entry coupons—and the more coupons you enter, the better your chances of winning!

© 1991 HARLEQUIN ENTERPRISES LTD.   2N-CPS